# THE COMPANY OF GLORY

Edgar Pangborn

KU-415-556

**A STAR BOOK**

*published by*

WYNDHAM PUBLICATIONS

A Star Book
Published in 1976
by Wyndham Publications Ltd
A Howard & Wyndham Company
123 King Street, London W6 9JG

First published in the United States by
Pyramid Communications Inc., 1975

Printed in Great Britain by
Richard Clay (The Chaucer Press), Ltd., Bungay, Suffolk

ISBN 0 352 39769 1

# CHAPTER ONE

## There will be Love in it

*If I missed my other glimpses of infinity I may find it
in a blade of grass.*

*DEMETRIOS.*

The old man swung his walnut stick, enjoying the heft
of it but not dependent on it; he was no more blind than
Homer. Ambling down Harrow Street, he encountered a
boy leading a horse to the blacksmith, and some girls who
had toiled up from the creek with laundry baskets. "A good
day to you, Garth! How's Frankie?"

"And to you, Demetrios," the boy said, smiling with
warmth and shyness. "Frankie, he's fine." Garth stood idle,
rubbing his horse's neck, watchful of the girls in their
damp smocks, who had set down their baskets and were
poking at their hair, but he was mindful of the old man
too. No one ignored the storyteller.

Demetrios's peregrine face appeared to fly toward you
even when motionless. His long right hand, prominent in
the joints, might rest on his walnut staff and still point
toward the outlands, the foreign visions. Demetrios stood
tall—advantageous for one gazing over preoccupied heads.
His gray hair, lightly silvered, fell straight to his shoulders.
He was sixty, not old but seasoned, like his walnut stick,
like a wine held long enough in the cask to have ripened
in a way that might not suit everyone. The boy Garth,
at an age when a good heart's love must flow outward,
adored him—what other ancient would remember a stable-
boy's name and his little brother too? And some were
caught by Demetrios's professional skill as a storyteller,
neither liking nor disliking him, but granting some tribute

5

of listening. A girl named Solitaire desired him and was desired.

From a side street a peddler, a ragpicker older than Demetrios, pushed his two-wheel barrow near them and rested it on its one-leg stand, mopping his face with a grimy cloth. The afternoon hung heavy with July; a wind heaving gray masses through the mountain air was not felt here, not yet, though before long a thunderstorm might drop on the meager makeshift town, stirring the mud, trash, and sewage in Nuber's streets and flushing a portion of the filth down the channels of the central ditches, shifting corruption from one spot to another as human society has done so long, so long. Time-beaten himself and practiced in impudence (any publicity is good publicity, they used to say in Old Time, so I'm told, until they choked on it) the peddler felt privileged to croak: "Dimmy, you old blast of wind! Got a story for us—one with balls to it?"

"Yours hanging low, Potterfield?" Demetrios's softer tone could have been heard sixty feet down the block. One of the girls giggled, spreading a laundry-pink hand over her mouth and watching Garth, who blushed easily; he wasn't over fifteen. Raised to reach the back row of a crowd, Demetrios's baritone sometimes sounded high in pitch. He had sung a little once, until a musician told him his ear was not quite true; his voice was better for spoken dreams. A woman leaned generously from a first-floor window with a dustcloth over her hair, and Demetrios asked: "May I sit myself here, Mam, while I tell you a tale of some sort if you want one?"

"The ssph—" she spat a peach pit into the sunken entryway below her window, and settled herself—"the steps a'n't ourn, we only rent. Sit anyhow and tell your tale, dear soul. I'll fight any sunny-bitch says you can't."

"So maybe I'll make it a tale for you, yourself it is, and there will be love in it, and Potterfield must put up with it."

"I got no cause against love," grumbled Potterfield, "as the fly said when his poor arse got jammed into the honey."

Demetrios sat in the shade and rested his hands on the knob of his walnut stick, and shut his eyes a summoning

6

while, watching the midnight ocean of memory and reflection for whatever cargo might seek the industrious wharves and warehouses of his mind. He knew a familiar fear, that on this day no ships had sailed: such days do arrive to afflict us. "I was a child," he said. "I think I've told no tales of childhood. There was once—no, not that one. Let me mull it over. Wind's in the east—that's not one of the fair-blowing winds. . . . All stories begin in childhood. Before speech.

"Hear then that I who talk to you was born in a small town that might seem large to you. Its population was about three thousand before the Twenty-Minute War, which marks the Year One of our calendar, and I suppose the present population here in the city of Nuber is hardly more than that—four thousand possibly, four thousand loyal subjects of the King's republic," he said, and nobody laughed.

"My birth-town was named Hesterville, and it was not many miles up a great river from the city of Hannibal in what was the state of Missouri. Missouri's a long way west —no matter if you never heard of it. A man named Sam Clemens was born at Hannibal, by the way, one hundred and forty-five years before my birth at Hesterville. I think of him because he was a storyteller too, but a great one. His tales were written in books, the books multiplied to thousands—that's called printing and you've heard of it; I'm told there's a hand press here at Nuber, I mean another besides the legal one they use in the Inner City. So Clemens's stories were read and preserved all over the world, which was larger then, dear souls, and quite round. He wrote them under the invented name of Mark Twain, better known than his original name. Names are important: with them we can talk to each other, a little. Mark Twain's stories will last, unless all books are lost and destroyed; even then bits of them will be told for a while. My stories are written on the air. Who knows where a story goes after the poet gives it to the winds?"

Then, I know, the old man brooded, whether to give them some of Huck Finn's tale—*The contexts are gone. There was a slavery in 1993, but the method and the idiom of it were altogether different. It was supervised by po-*

7

*faced experts who gave it the name of Temporary Suspension of Normalcy. What could these ignorant friendly folk make of openly admitted slavery? Or of Nigger Jim? "All right, I'll GO to Hell!"—what could they make of that? Contexts gone. As for Huck's antebellum world, lost so long ago that even to my boyhood reading it seemed remoter than Pan's Arcadia—why, of that they might understand a little if I could transmit it to them. It is nearer to us than it was at any time in the 20th Century. now that the flabby plastic carcass of industrialism is buried. Gradually the air loses that foulness; the earth, and even the tortured and degraded sea, begin to regain some of the beauty that dollar-progress ravaged and smeared. There's loss too. So be it. If I missed my other glimpses of infinity I may find it in a blade of grass.*

He knew he had been keeping silent too long. He opened his eyes and beamed on his audience with a practiced shrewdness, to let them know he had not dozed off senile and forgetful. They were attentive; one or two smiled back. Others had strolled up during his abstraction; he had been aware of their coming but had wanted to follow his thought further. In a time when literacy is rare the storyteller and newsbearer come into their own; and the memories of some listeners develop astonishing powers that an age of typewriter and newspaper must have lost or submerged. Demetrios studied the little crowd, some of the faces dubiously familiar but all without names except the plump sweet face of Garth.

In the canvas cap that he had dropped upside down near his feet a few coins were lying. Most of these were the brass pennies of the King's Republic of Katskil, crudely stamped with the slab-jawed face of Brian II. (Like his father Brian I, he called his monarchy a Provisional Government, its holy aim the restoration of the United States of America, which alas was not quite practical right *now*.) Among the pennies shone a startling fragment of the past, accepted legal tender but a great rarity, an Old-Time silver dime worth at least fifty of the Katskil pennies. Who in this group would have been that munificent?

8

It was almost certainly the dark-haired youth who sat apart from the rest holding the leash of a gray wolfhound. His linen tunic and loincloth were cream-white, unofficial sign of the aristocracy; though not a matter of law, none but they wore the expensive bleached linen in public; commoners put up with clothes slung together by the inexpert housewife or sweatshop serf from ill-woven drab-colored wool, or linsey-woolsey—wool and linen remnants and scraps. The aristocracy took pride in cleanness, while on some levels dirt was equated with virtue. This youth's deerhide hip satchel and moccasins would have been made by the bonded servants, virtually slaves, who did such labor for the Inner City and the large estates in the suburbs. The boy's direct and innocent gaze troubled Demetrios, who was haunted by another world dead for nearly half a century. "I think a story goes wherever there's a spark of hearing life. In Hesterville we had those devices that seem fairy-tale fancies to anyone too young to have seen them. Nobody here except Potterfield would recall them as I do—telephones, automobiles, radio, earth-moving machines, aircraft. Naturally you find it hard to believe in them. Remember space flight, Potterfield?"

"Shit," said the peddler. "Made that one up, di'n't they? I never seen no sacklite go up except like on the teevy same as them other space-opries with made-up people."

"What happened to your teevy?" asked the dark-haired boy.

"Busted," said Potterfield. "Busted, sir. See, when the power went bleh, wouldn't nothing work." He winked at Demetrios, sharing an ancient half-wisdom gone useless and sour. "So my girl friend flang a bottle of hand lotion into it—an empty one. Was her teevy actually. Was shacking up with her at the time, fifty years ago nearabout. I'm seventy now by Jesus, since you ask."

"You remember the cars too," said Demetrios. "Remember the telephones? Jet planes?"

"Of course. Even now if I have to gosemplace I think, oh, I'll just phone, and then I think, well, shit." Potterfield scratched under his soggy loin-rag, irritated by many griefs, old age not the least of them. Crablice, rats, and fleas had survived the long-ago holocaust abundantly. During the

9

last two or three decades, as the risen waters held their level with only slight fluctuations, a small, aggressive variety of short-tailed rat was doing especially well—dark-pelted, savage, with a liking for the new cheap human dwellings that were no longer built set up on concrete foundations. It might be a sport from the prolific meadow-mouse of Old Time, Demetrios thought, but there was no one to discuss it with him who would even know the word "genetics." "Better off, ain't we?" said Potterfield. He would have been about twenty, Demetrios reflected, when fire scourged the cities and the short plagues followed, radiation deaths and epidemics of crushing virulence with no means for study or control. The great Red Plague did not come until sixteen years later, when Demetrios was twenty-nine, and living at Nuber. Potterfield must have been a simple young man (if any human being ever answered that description) with a hunger for simple satisfactions (if there are any satisfactions that don't spread like pond ripples to infinity). There had been so many like him! Male and female of all ages, passing four billion by the estimates of 1990, in spite of a slight drop in the birthrate and the desolating famines of the late 1970s and early 1980s. "Better off, not so much crap all the time flying at you. Man has a chance to think," said Potterfield. "You wouldn't believe the amount of deep thinking I get through nowadays. Get on with your story, Dimmy—I set down here to be entertained, didn't I?"

"You shall be, if you stay awake. I grew up in that world," said Demetrios, "to the age of thirteen, not comfortable, for nobody was then except the unthinking who can be comfortable on the side of a volcano. Being a child, of course I was often unthinking too. I—"

"Aw, Demetrios!" The woman in the window had finished her peach and wiped her mouth on her arm. "Volcano? You got to use all them big words? What's a volcano?"

"Sorry, Mam. A volcano is a mountain with a hole in its top. From time to time the hole lets out the fire of the earth, in a molten river that rolls down the mountain burning everything. Did you know, my darling, the inside of the earth is a core of fire? Every day you walk above a

10

cellar of *fire*, my darling. Now no more questions or I stop my tale." But it was the boy Garth who showed alarm, and even glanced sheepishly down toward his feet; the woman was only amused and not believing. "Yes, I grew up in that world, my father a doctor and a wise man. My mother was a painter of pictures. There are some in Nuber; she was more skillful than any you know—and had better materials to work with, of course. My father was known as Dr. Isaac Freeman of Hesterville, and my name—why, my name was Adam Freeman. I have not told of these things before." *And what comes over you now, to go so falteringly toward the telling of them? They don't want this, Demetrios. They want romances, fairy tales, even allegory if you're careful—words to ease the sting of daily hardships, but certainly not the story of how things really were! Well, the wind is in the east.* "I must feel my way, dear souls. My name was not then Demetrios. It was Adam Freeman.

"My name has been Demetrios for forty-seven years —long enough to have seen these near waters rise and become the Hudson Sea. I have beheld one more messiah, seventeen years ago, and his martyrdom by those he sought to save. I speak of the man Abraham whom some call prophet, bound on the wheel in Gallows Square of this town."

"Was he not a prophet?" asked the youth with the wolf-hound. "I'm sorry—I didn't mean to interrupt."

"All men are prophets," said Demetrios, studying him. His presence here was only a little odd. Citizens of the Inner City, who could go wherever they pleased, were not uncommonly seen in the open streets, especially with pro-tecting dogs or servants, and though they seldom bothered to pause for streetcorner storytellers, there was no reason to wonder at it. "And since men never agree, perhaps no man should have the name. My name is Demetrios. It means 'belonging to the earth'—'sacred to the earth.' In ancient times a goddess Demeter was worshiped as the spirit of the earth, the all-mother—worshiped under other names too. Demeter was the name given her by the Greeks—you know of them, sir?"

The boy looked bothered, perhaps by the "sir" from one

11

so much older; but most people wearing such linen would take it as their natural right. "I do know of them," he said, and smiled, not arrogantly. "I know some of the books."

Demetrios nodded. "Then you will have found there's life in them. I am Demetrios. If anyone called me on the street by that name *Adam Freeman* I might not understand it was meant for me. My father used to call me Ad; to my mother, who was Welsh, I was Adam-bach.

"I was thirteen in the year 1993, old calendar. Now remember, dear souls, a whole continent extends to the west, north, and south of here—what the ocean hasn't submerged—and in that region our entire nation of Katskil would amount to a fingernail wedge of dirt on a big blanket. That's the vast region you're speaking of when you say 'United States of America.' Up to the year 1993, after which there's no written history we know of except for our little fingernail wedge, the rest of the world was marked off into other territorial divisions large and small —maybe it still is, but no one speaks across the oceans any more. Those divisions all called themselves nations, and were quite free to make war on each other with weapons that could turn the earth into a slag-heap—as it is today any more. Those divisions all called themselves *nations* and alliances of nations, dear souls, have not the mother wit to avoid the stupid passion of war. Nations are no more capable of justice or charity than of love, for they are, essentially, organized crowds. Individual persons can love and be loved; they can be generous and kind, forbearing, even brave; nations, never. A crowd can neither think nor feel. Thinking is lonely work, dear souls, and feeling is the experience of the separate heart."

A close-faced man among the listeners made up his mind about something and walked away. His lingering image annoyed Demetrios; his features would have been hard to swear to on a second meeting—neutral, bland, cold.

"In 1993, at thirteen, I was reading the scanty censored newspaper from Chicago for what emerged between the lines, with my father's grim interpretations. We—my parents who treated me like a grown-up and I—we learned from radio and television what we were expected to think,

12

so that we could appear to think it in the presence of strangers. We knew—"

"Look," said Potterfield, "you ain't telling no story, you're just beating your gums about old times—who needs it?"

"Ah, Potterfield! Once upon a time there were two little married people named Adam and Eve, and they had two little boys, one named Cain and—"

"Oh, *shit!* Forget I said anything."

"We knew the war would come, and in 1993 it came: the 24th day of June 1993—according to an old religion which was even then rapidly fading, that was the day of St. John the Baptist, though I can't say whether anyone noticed it. The Twenty-Minute War we call it now, though actually I remember seeing a bomb-flare over the horizon on the second night. It's impossible to say which major division of the world had elected to try for suicide. We—"

"Why," said Potterfield, "it was the Russians."

"So you were told automatically by the teevy until the power went off. I remember a broadcast from South America on our car radio, accusing us. The battery radio soon ran down, then the big silence. My guess is that the United States touched off the final lunacy, but does it matter now? Other nations were almost as rotten-ripe, the whole society watergated—"

"Hell!" Potterfield lurched to his feet and grabbed the handle of his cart. "I won't sit around listening to no such wickedness as that." He rattled away, halting at the corner to thrust his hand toward Demetrios, fingers pronged against the evil eye.

Mainly for the dark-haired boy, Demetrios remarked: "There goes maybe the last American patriot." One of the four laundry girls got up to go, but her companion checked her dubiously.

Garth let his old plug clump a step or two nearer. "Old Potterfield never had no sense."

"Aye," said Demetrios, "that's what makes him different from you and me." The woman in the window seemed undisturbed. "The bombs were for the great cities and launching areas. One direct hit obliterated Chicago, two hundred and fifty miles from Hesterville. The bombs were of the

13

kind described, in the insane jargon of the age, as 'clean.' This meant simply that they killed more people by impact and fire than by a poisoning of the atmosphere that the senders of the bombs might have found inconvenient —for they had persistent delusions about staying alive while they defended freedom or whatever the hell they were doing. I suppose all through history people have imagined that giving horror a pretty name makes it no longer horror.

"I have made up my mind. I will tell you how I acquired the name of Demetrios, and only that story. Never mind the cars, airplanes, bombs, all that trash. You've heard of it before: let it rust. And bear with me: in order to tell the story about my name I must say a little more about the ending of Old Time.

"There were the short plagues, sicknesses that raged for a few days and passed like firestorms, leaving their dead. Different from the radiation deaths."

"Red Plague?" said the dark-haired boy.

"No, that came sixteen years later, only—let me think —thirty-one years ago. No, the short plagues—they may have come from the war laboratories, our own, likely, torn apart and scattered. Such methods of warfare were supposed to have been discontinued much earlier, but that happy announcement had been made by a government that lied about virtually all its other activities, and later —this was before my time—later it developed that the Pentagon's only concern was to develop gases and diseases that would be safe for the users to handle—you know, *clean* ways of destroying other people who were so inconsiderate as to be foreigners."

"Pentagon?"

"Oh—that was the nightmare building in the city of Washington that housed the war machine—called, of course, the Defense Department. Yes, I think it's likely the short plagues were man-made, but you understand, there was neither time nor means to study them when they were destroying us. Certainly the military mind is incapable of abandoning such toys.

"We let that mind win, by default. We overpopulated the earth, spawning to the point of famine, exhausting

14

natural resources with no restraint, no thought for future needs, and piling up corruption. Our breed grew like a tumor. The surgery that ended the overgrowth was performed, not by reason as it might have been, but by famine, pestilence, and a war of idiots."

Round-eyed and indignant, the laundry girl who wanted to go snatched up her basket and dragged her friend along with her. If the people of Nuber believed anything in these years, they believed that the King's Republic was engaged in the imminent restoration of the United States of America and the Golden Age. But the other two girls lingered, and Garth, and a tired friendly-faced woman with a market basket, and a young couple hand in hand who might not have been listening much, and the dark-haired boy with the wolfhound. The dog stretched and yawned open his fearsome teeth, laughing with a big pink tongue.

"And that surgery was presently aided," said Demetrios, "by the sterility and birth deformities brought on by radiation—from atomic industry as well as weapons—which may pursue us for another thousand years, or five thousand, if we can last that long."

"I bore a mue two years ago," said the woman in the window. "He had no anus. Lived a day. I ha'n't conceived since. Nor tried to prevent it. My husband says it's all God's punishment on us."

"A woman who was like a wife to me long ago," said Demetrios, "Elizabeth of Hartford, conceived a mue with a swollen eggshell skull. It cracked during the delivery that destroyed her own life. Now what do you imagine you did to be so punished, Mam?"

"We don't know. My husband says it'll all be explained with the coming of the Messiah, and he could come like anybody, you know. Like that Abraham. Like you, yourself it is."

"Nay-nay, I'm a rusty storyteller, nothing more."

"Then get on with the story about your name, dear soul."

CHAPTER TWO

## A Music of Surviving Birds

*. . . For as this appalling ocean surrounds the verdant
land, so in the soul of man there lies one insular
Tahiti, full of peace and joy, but encompassed by all
the horrors of the half-known life.*
                    —*Herman Melville, MOBY DICK.*

"My name is Demetrios.

"My father and mother died within hours of each other,
in coma following a few hours of paroxysmal cramps and
high fever—I have no name for the sickness. In the uncanny manner of the short plagues, I was untouched,
though death prevailed all around me and hardly any were
left to attempt the burials. Perhaps I and a few others had
a light infection of the same thing, whatever it was. That's
only speculation, for science as men had known it was
ended. Civilization ended with a writhing in the streets
and a stillness.

"Hesterville had been a town of about three thousand.
A few weeks after the Twenty-Minute War I don't suppose more than five hundred were left alive. Can you
imagine the empty houses and the reek of death? A hot
July: the earth steamed to the sun through short inter-
missions of intolerable rains—those rains!—but it was
hot rain that did nothing to lighten the corruption it could
not wash away. A listless, sodden, windless rain; the sky
was bleeding water like a sacrifice.

"One person left alone, as I was, could survive only as
a slinking animal. Food was where you found it, all
shadows a threat and all strangers. Our house where my
parents lay dead was looted by a gang of half a dozen

16

louts who ran through the remnants of our town like a twister off the plains. I escaped them unseen. Later I saw a couple of them shot down from a window by someone with a repeating rifle, who I suppose took the law on himself because it existed nowhere else; they twitched a while under the rain.

"Hesterville—why, I think it's under water now. Sometimes a dream takes me to it, a place of whitened bones; once, in that way, I found it a place of seaweed wavering, swaying over a white statue that stood benign but unanswering in the green depth—it looked like my mother, and I would have embraced it but the water held me away like impenetrable glass.

"The day after I escaped the looters I took the road out of Hesterville, without a goal and hungry. Government, I knew, did not exist. You know most of the important things at thirteen—the rest is comment and filling-in. Can I make it understandable? You and I, all of us, dear souls, are used to government of a sort here at Nuber, maybe too much. There's been more continuity here than in most places, ever since the Twenty-Minute War and the other disasters. People preserve government in some form because they must. True anarchy's intolerable: the wolves, the wild deer, don't live in anarchy, they follow strict laws, some of them even self-imposed, and the lawbreakers usually perish. Well, forty-seven years ago, at Hesterville and a million other places, government for a short while was wholly smashed, a gone mechanism. I escaped into a nearly silent world, but I knew that wherever I should encounter human eyes hell might be simmering behind them.

"I walked some miles before I came on a car slantwise across the road—I'm speaking of an Old-Time motor vehicle, an automobile. Cars were no longer numerous in 1993; the great swarm of them was before my time. The seventy-year gasoline joyride sputtered out to a silly finish in the 1970s; alternative methods were developing, and could have amounted to something in time but got off to a bad start, partly because the oil and automobile companies had too long prevented any rational trial and research along that line, partly because of a general sag of energy—I mean human energy. What we called civilization had pretty well worn us out. . . . In that stalled car a well-dressed man was slumped lifeless across the wheel and there was a dead baby in the rear seat. Sickness must have struck him while he drove—no mark of violence. He may have hoped that being on the move would help; Americans used to believe that activity, however aimless and wrongheaded, must be a good in itself. The bodies were not convulsed. That had passed for my people also, during the coma; I think those two died from the same destroyer. Once sentient flesh, they had come to a certain position in time and space, and there ceased, with quiet faces. I took some of the food I found in the car. I remember a music of surviving birds."

"Bless them!" said the woman in the window.

"Yes, in 1993 nonhuman life was recovering, here and there, from the ravages of industry. There was no such morning music as we can enjoy now, but they sang. In forty-seven years, Mam, I think a few more species have died out from the long-lasting poisons, but others have survived and multiplied. In our vanity we still imagine it's for us they sing. I wish there were robins.

"Later that day I heard a bell tinkle behind me when the rain was briefly quieting, and a boy and girl rode up on bicycles. They were fresh-faced and kind, and after a first stare, not afraid of me. The girl said: 'We're friends, man—don't be spookered.' They were, and remained so. That was Laura Wilmot, and the boy was George Wilmot, her cousin. They were acting as advance scouts for a group of seven people who were following the leadership of a rugged old man, Judd Wilmot—Laura's uncle, George's father—and they told me as soon as they knew I was alone, without any other questioning, that I was one of them.

"Their kindness broke me down. 'Why, cry it out!' says Laura, and opened her raincoat and mine, to hug me. 'What's your name?' 'Adam,' I said. 'Well, dear Father Adam,' said Laura, to make me laugh; and George, who never said much, was making kind noises. I was a small snip of thirteen just beginning a spurt of growth. George was nineteen I think, large and bland.

"Judd Wilmot I would call a natural commander. He also was kind, in his own fashion, and possessed organizing sense, ability to guide and give orders. Fanatic: an idea once stuck in his skull couldn't be dislodged. One of these ideas was a conviction, heaven knows the source, that things must be better to the east of us, and he would prove it if it meant going all the way to the Atlantic and jumping in. He could be severe, as a commander must, and either he never had any sense of humor or it was shocked out of him by the horrors of the time. I never knew him to be mean or stupid or unjust.

"There was Judd's wife Miranda, soft and self-effacing, and Judd's gloomy younger brother Howard who was Laura's father, a widow named Andromache Makarios— she had been a neighbor of the Wilmots in their Kansas town—and Andromache's eighteen-year-old son Demetrios.

"Within a few months, by the way, those bicycles were as useless as the cars. Tires and bearings—no replacements. Last drop of machine oil—no replacement. That's how a world ran down, in a clutter of midget failures after the large ones, leaving us more helpless than people of ancient times who never dreamed of an industrial age.

"Andromache was lonely and passionate, perhaps always had been. Her husband, one of the few who still tried to live by farming instead of mining the exhausted earth for dollars, had died on the day of the Twenty-Minute War— of a heart attack. Like all who survived the disasters including myself, she was still in shock. I remember more than once she fell behind, and halting for her we saw her just standing with her face uplifted to the rain; and Judd, or Demetrios, would go back to rouse her from the partial trance. She had not given up, and would not while she could cling to Demetrios, and Demetrios at eighteen understood that. After we became friends he told me he had been on the point of leaving home, longing to, breaking the chains of gossamer as he called it himself, a son's necessary escape. His father had been well able to care for fey Andromache, and wanted him to go for his own sake; but now that comprehending man was dead, and so was the world.

"How shall I give you an image of that Demetrios who

was my friend, who seemed so marvelously old to me then and now would seem like a boy? Judd and Howard both commented on a likeness between us as strong as if we had been brothers, though Laura said she couldn't see it. We were both dark, with this straight high-bridged nose and full underlip; maybe that's all it amounted to. When I remember his face I see no image of myself, but another person whom I loved as a very separate being.

"Andromache and I from our first meeting were uneasy with each other. What she felt I've never known; what I felt was a tension that affected me like hostility, but may have been nothing of the kind. Dark and small she was, and must have been approaching forty, though in her girlish slenderness she looked to me hardly any older than wonderful Demetrios.

"I think Judd Wilmot was very little aware of the complex of emotions—not all of them young emotions—that swirled among us. We were caught up in his own fantasy about the eastern states—dear man, he'd been born in Vermont, though only five when his family moved west— because we had no stronger contrary notions and no such force of determination. Out of love and respect for him, we stayed on our good behavior in his presence. Antique he was, prudish, almost like a survival from the 19th Century of Old Time, or rather from what I imagine the 19th Century to have been.

"Demetrios, before the crash, had determined to become a motion picture director. That meant the one who planned and managed the creation of those images in motion— you will have heard of them and I won't stop to explain how photography worked, though I did understand it once —which provided a great part of the entertainment of 20th Century people. In my boyhood, motion pictures had established the possibilities of a great art form, the only one the industrial age originated, in fact the only basic innovation in the arts since the start of oil painting in the late Middle Ages, and the early working out of systems of harmony and counterpoint at about the same time. Demetrios grasped these possibilities. He was a youth, he had grown up on a Kansas farm (but his farmer father was well read), and he had seen movies mainly through the medium of the teevy. But still he sensed the vast area of dramatic art that had to exist behind the poverty of what he saw in the corrupted boob tube, and his heart had been set on entering that world of creation and liberating his own fresh marvels in it. He could have done it, I think.

"When I met him and made a hero out of him, he was not accepting the wreck of our society as a final thing. Rational about everything else, he clung somehow to a quite irrational conviction that when our people restored the framework of society, the complex of mechanical production that supported the making of motion pictures would naturally be reactivated along with it. He forgot (and I was no wiser) that the cinema was the only major art that depended for its existence on the sophisticated engineering of an industrial age. There can be great music without pianos or complex keyed wind instruments. Give a painter or sculptor his basic materials, however crude, and the visual arts can live. But Demetrios's art had been cut at the roots. Understanding the creative side, he had scant knowledge of the engineering aspect—hadn't looked into it yet, he told me; knowing less than he did, I took his word for that, and went along unquestioning. I see now that he probably knew better: it was a willful blindness.

"Worshiping his least word, I was happy to fling myself into—well, we called them rehearsals, and often had the half-reluctant help of George and Laura. Occasionally Andromache got into them too, at Demetrios's begging, but inevitably she conveyed an impression of humoring the child, allowing her sad amusement to be glimpsed. Like many mothers she loved her son, with little or no respect for him.

"Demetrios would direct us out of his one-volume Shakespeare, our only book on that journey. He would storm at us and labor over our performance of what we barely understood, with fierce insistence on the reality of dramatic illusion. To him (and to me) Macbeth, Lear, Rosalind, Falstaff, all the glorious company were as real as Judd or George or Laura or myself; more real, because immortal.

21

I still like to think, dear souls, that Hamlet's perplexities will be under discussion long after I'm dead.

"So, like a company of players without an audience, we groped our way from Missouri as far as Pennsylvania—it took us two months, well into September, but it's true we had no reason for haste—before anything happened to burst the bubble of Demetrios's dream. Maybe some of the intensity he brought to those rehearsals was appropriate to an earlier phase of youth; solemn folk, like Howard Wilmot, would say he should have grown up sooner. But if it resembled a child's fantasy it was carried out with the prodigal passion of an adolescent who was in most respects a man, and an artist from the heart out.

"In a way, I hold Howard Wilmot to blame, yet according to his lights what he did was well meant. Judd, though I don't think he would have done it himself, did nothing to prevent it, only stood by and let it happen, not understanding until too late.

"We were in a town somewhere near Harrisburg, a wholly deserted town where a soft insistent southwest wind was driving the rain down along the desolation of Main Street, a swarm of silver ghosts. The little town was all ours to do with as we chose; in that September it was still possible to find canned stuff in the groceries or the forsaken dwellings, though perhaps in the company of the disintegrating dead. In that valley town, though—I remember the name of it, it was Aberedo—everything had been left tidy. Perhaps the survivors of plagues and war had abandoned it in fear of flood, for a river ran through the place, roaring high to the banks—and had chosen to leave their bit of the world in good order. We took refuge from the rain as we had done at many other towns, in a public building. It was a motion picture theater, and it was Howard who suggested it.

"We had used one before, much earlier, when Demetrios and I had explored the place top to bottom, and used the stage area for a rehearsal of *Othello;* but this time Howard took it on himself to show Demetrios. He steered us up to the projection booth, and made it all his show—Judd was there, and Andromache came too, and Howard lectured with the obdurate wisdom of a garage mechanic.

'This here is a reel, Demmy,' he said. 'That there is a projector—look at the damn thing, more parts than a fine car.' Howard was fed up with the rehearsals; they bothered him; they were a waste of time—though I don't know what he hoped to do with the time saved—and I think he also felt that some of the language in Shakespeare wasn't quite nice. 'This here box 'that holds the projection lamp, see, this is a real special metal, built to stand heat. I been told the heat of them lamps is a caution, and they was pretty special too, I don't guess there'd be a soul alive knows how to make one, supposing he had the makings. See, it ain't like this, now, organic gardening, I mean a man can take a piece of land and grow things, but see, there ain't no living to be made out of this.' He was trying to be kind, or thought he was, and I hadn't the courage to tell him to shut up. 'See, Demmy, you take that reel of film for instance, you know what that film is made of? Plastic. You know what plastic is made of? It's a p'troleum product. All plastics is p'troleum products,' said Howard, who had read an article about it. 'Thing of it is, Demmy, moo'n' pictures has had it. Of course, so long as it's just a game—'

" 'Well,' said my friend agreeably, 'I will cease my games.' And he went down into the theater, walking naturally, no one with him but me, and I felt his pain in a way that made it impossible for me to speak. Then he was hurrying to the door, and out in the rain, and running, and I ran after him, but I couldn't keep up to him, I couldn't make him stop by screaming to him, he ran out on the bridge over the muddy torrent of the river, and climbed the rail, and was gone. He couldn't swim. I could; I kicked off my shoes and went in after him—hopeless of course, the current had wrenched him far downstream, and down. I must have wanted to die myself, or I wouldn't have been foolish enough to try it; then I suppose the natural animal part of me was not ready to die. I remember catching hold of something, a timber I guess, and forcing my way somehow to the bank a quarter-mile or so downstream, where George and Judd found me and carried me home. I wasn't unconscious, just exhausted. I knew all about it when Andromache flung herself on me and kissed me and cried: 'O Demetrios—thank God, Demetrios! Poor Adam's gone, then? Demetrios, I'm so *sorry!* I know how you loved him, Demetrios, I know.'

"I think Judd Wilmot said: 'Andromache, God is not mocked.' But that was the only time he reproved her, seeing that the rest of us had said nothing, and I don't think she heard it at all.

"She never relinquished the illusion, and from the start we had been used to softening everything for Andromache. It was for myself a kind of madness, if you like, to take the name of someone I had loved so much, and in a way become that person, but—one grows accustomed, even to madness. It seemed to take away nothing from the ancient part of life that was Hesterville; I even imagined my real mother approving of what I did. We came on, we settled here at Nuber where a working order was already established, and stayed together as a group for a short while, about six months I think it was, before Andromache died. Then Judd elected to take the rest on to Vermont—he never liked Nuber, found it godless—but I elected to remain here and have done so ever since, telling you stories from time to time, and earning my living as a respectable janitor.

"Andromache had one other trouble of the mind—more than one, but one that I'll tell you about because it seems to be part of the story. She had never read books—for her the teevy took the place of them. But some legends out of books had come to her, and woke her curious power of belief. After I had become Demetrios, or Demetrios had become myself—I don't know what way I should say it—Andromache spoke a great deal about Tom Sawyer, as if he were someone she had known until recently; but in her mind Mark Twain's great creation strayed far from the original, taking on qualities of Lancelot and the dead Demetrios and Jesus. Here at Nuber she sat about and daydreamed a great deal; she did not talk aloud to Tom Sawyer, but her expression would shift and change in a thousand ways as if she carried on a conversation with everything but voice. And often she wandered away, but never got into trouble and always came back—we grew careless. She became interested in collecting herbs, and

24

would bring back basketfuls of this and that, usually dandelion or plantain or similar good harmless things, but one day she brought in some pure white umbrella-shaped mushrooms. 'Dear God!' says Judd's wife Miranda, 'them's death-caps, you mustn't touch them things, Andy, good heavens!' 'Oh,' said Andromache, 'are they bad? Throw them out then,' she said, and giggled. 'If they're bad we can't serve them when Tom Sawyer comes tomorrow, I think he said tomorrow.' And two days later she was talking to me in the cautious way she did, never looking me full in the face but repeatedly calling me Demetrios, when she became violently sick. Why, when she was talking with Miranda she must have already eaten some death-caps—raw, I suppose, in the field.

"I never thought of becoming Adam Freeman again. Laura hesitantly called me Adam, a day after Andromache died; I shook my head. A sweet soul, Laura. I often wished we were closer, but the two-world she had with George was an old-fashioned kind that could make no room for a third. I am Demetrios—aye-so, and surely, for the janitor of a sex-house, Demetrios is a better name than Adam."

Behind his eyes Demetrios wished they would go. It had not been their kind of story—nor his, for that matter: it seemed to him he could tell dreams better than truth, whatever truth is. It had been forced from him without his conscious art, by the power of memory. He felt the sultry breeze, and his own weariness.

"Sir?"

"Yes, Garth?"

"I just wondered if you was going to tell us more."

"Nay, no more. I dreamed last night that I was traveling west on a railroad, behind a steam locomotive with a big-bellied smokestack, something I never saw myself except in pictures. Long strings of cars there were, pulled along parallel steel tracks, they called them rails. There might be rusted remnants of those rails, here and there in the woods—nay, no more."

"My aunt has the sight—you know? She can read too, Demetrios. She's got this dream book where she says it tells like all what them things mean. I could ask her to look in it about yours."

"She might say I ought to make my westward journey."

"Once she told me out of the book how you could make like true dreams by putting rosemary and, well, things, under your pillow, I mean I did that and there was one, a you-know, one of those dreams, it was real great."

"They say it's wilderness now," said the young man with the wolfhound, "all the way west from Penn to some ocean —would that be what they called the Pacific, sir?"

"Might be," said Demetrios. "But since the Hudson has risen to become an inland sea, the Mississippi must have done the same, so that's likely the ocean they mean. An amazing rise, you know, for so short a time as half a century. At the Nuber waterfront they tell me the level's kept steady now for about five years. An inland sea would put Hesterville under water. Not much high ground there. Might be small islands."

Behind him someone asked: "Got a license for story-telling?"

The youth with the wolfhound stood up, murmuring reassurance to the rangy beast. Garth was viewing the newcomer, hands firm by the horse's head, his innocence suddenly shuttered behind blue eyes that looked older and dangerous. Demetrios turned his head without haste. The policeman had come softly in his moccasins, a stodgy decent soul known to Demetrios, in the uniform of dark blue loincloth and shirt with embroidered gold circle, his club at his belt. "They want a license for it now, Joe?"

"If you do it on the street. Constitutes collecting a crowd."

"Joe, I've been yarning on the streetcorners for at least fifteen years and you know it. You've stopped to listen yourself sometimes." Joe's embarrassment was a skim of ice on a pond in early frost. "It's my living, Joe, apart from janitor work."

"Ain't been on the books long, sir. I won't take you in— we don't want no trouble. Only you got to get a license before you do it again. See about it at the Town Hall."

"What does it cost?"

Joe cleared his throat and looked away. "Ask 'em at the Town Hall, ain't my department. Let's break it up, folks. No subversion. Can't have no crowds on Harrow Street."

"Joe Park," said the woman in the window, "you son of a bitch."

"Move on, folks. Break it up. We don't want no trouble."

# CHAPTER THREE

## But What Is Peace?

> Knowledge enormous makes a god of me.
> Names, deeds, grey legends, dire events, rebellions,
> Majesties, sovran voices, agonies,
> Creations and destroyings, all at once
> Pour into the wide hollows of my brain . . .
> —*Keats, HYPERION.*

The listeners dispersed. Demetrios tried to remember when that close-faced fellow had slipped away; it had been after those remarks about nations, persons, crowds, which might stir up that man's superiors—who would be at Inner City, he supposed.

As a good janitor, Demetrios wished to be law-abiding if only the law would show some sense. He had not the inner clench, akin to despair and vanity, that squeezes the revolutionary's mind. The police of the city-state of Nuber did not frighten Demetrios. He had rarely seen them misbehave. To be sure, he did not have a true worm's-eye view of them. In boyhood he had not felt much of the understandable 20th Century American hatred for police; his father's shrewd and tranquil sense of humor had steered him away from other excesses too.

Patrolman Joe Park, duty done, marched away, flipping a hand toward the woman in the window to acknowledge her insult. Demetrios rose with stiffness; quickly, unobtrusively, Garth's hand aided him. The plowhorse snuffled at Demetrios's neck. Garth muttered: "I hate the stupid cops, could shit in their beer." From gentle Garth, the words startled. "One of 'em beat up on Frankie last week, and he hadn't done nothing, only pee a little on that statue

28

in the Meadows, the one near the entrance, I guess it's St. Franklin, with the spade jaw. Lots of people do—Frankie's only twelve; they didn't have to beat up on him."

"Brand here can't get by that damn statue," said the youth with the wolfhound. "I don't think he'd mind the leash if I tried to stop him, so usually I have a shot at it too." The dog wagged gratification at the music of his name. "I'm Angus Bridgeman, sir."

"Peace with you, Angus, yourself it is," said Demetrios. "My name you know." His weariness was dissolving, as if the warmth of the young could flow into old bones and joints. "I suppose we'd best move on, in case Joe's got eyes in his back. And I must get to the Town Hall—but not today. I'll go home; I'm tired. Mam, was it a story with enough love in it?"

"Well, there was love in it. I'd ask you all in for a cup-tea, but the house is a mess and my man'll soon be home."

"Another time. Bless you."

"And you, man Demetrios. You be good boys." They moved off down the street. The woman's face saddened as a field goes drab when sunlight abandons it to roving cloud; she turned back to the work of the world.

*—Here I who wrote this book must intrude an instant—no more than an instant I promise you and then I'm gone, out of sight—to say that this woman is no fiction (O stars in daytime, what is fiction?)—indeed, I stayed a day or two at her house on my last return to Nuber, and wasn't she full of peace and quiet and pregnant again, wouldn't you know it? Real, yes, but sensitive, does not wish her name to be used. Now I'm gone.—*

"I gosemplace here," said Garth at the next corner. "Then I'll ask my aunt to see the book about your dream, Demetrios?"

"Do, Garth," said Demetrios, loving him. "And tell me."

"You was traveling west on a—a rail train."

"Aye-so, and it may have passed Aberedo, but that thought only nudged me like an owl's shadow under the moon."

"I'll see you again around and about."

"Yes, Garth. Peace."

"Peace, Demetrios, Mister Bridgeman." Garth was gone,

his horse's hard steps receding with neat dry noise down Franklin Street, where bricks had replaced a decayed blacktop of Old Time. Harrow Street, with very little traffic of oxcarts and wagons, still had a usable amount of the ancient paving, its crumbled spots and frostholes occasionally repaired, by order of Town Hall, with a random fiurrup of dirt. Walking on with the quiet youth and his great gray dog, Demetrios brooded on the word *Peace*. One spoke it nowadays as we once said "So long" or "Be seeing you"—indeed, the usage had begun long ago, before 1993, but in the 20th Century it seems to have had pious overtones, an assumption that only the religious could know the meaning of peace. Now no one gave it a thought, as for centuries no one had remembered that "Good-bye" derived from "God be with you!" But what is peace? Something more than the absence of strife and confusion?

"Have you truly been a storyteller for fifteen years? That's more than three-quarters of my lifetime."

"It must be about fifteen, Angus Bridgeman. You're about nineteen, yourself it is?"

"Next month."

"Live in health. Yes, so far as Nuber is concerned, you could say I invented the profession of storytelling. The imitators flatter me—no, actually some are better than I am, I know."

"Isn't that false modesty? I don't think they are."

"Maybe." The boy's almost stern remark was like a tug at his arm. "There's a vanity goes with the storytelling profession. My father gave me an example of intellectual humility, rare in any doctor, I suppose, not to be found at all in today's quacks. But I have that vanity. One afternoon I was idle on a streetcorner, full of the myths of the world, and it just happened. I said: 'Hear me who speak to you—' my voice sounded good, presently I was telling the story of the Argonauts, with my own inventions . . . Are you kin to that Simon Bridgeman who was the true founder of Nuber?"

"Simon was my uncle, sixteen years older than my father who—who died last year. My father was only fourteen when Simon was assassinated, and Simon governed only a little over two years—isn't that right?—before the assassination."

"Yes, about two years. When I came here with Judd's party Simon Bridgeman had the new town already organized and was accepting refugees. Word got around, even in that confusion."

"I first heard your storytelling four years ago. It was at the corner of Broad and Dover streets, and I was fifteen. That was a July afternoon too but very hot, we were all sweating up a stink and you had drawn a good-sized crowd. I was with my father and so not free to—not free." Angus's voice was warm with the plangent overtones of late adolescence. Demetrios wondered whether the boy might have tactfully steered him away from the subject of the Bridgeman clan—too important in the Inner City, rumor said, for Brian II and his administration to wish conflict with them. "That time too it was the story of the Argonauts. You held me. I *was* Jason."

"The Greeks might hardly recognize it."

"Their hard luck. Are you in a hurry to get home, Demetrios?"

"Ah, it's a pleasant place with a dear woman in it, and I'm tired. I'm janitor at Mam Estelle's on Redcurtain Street —art is a noble profession, but one must eat. I would always have time for you, Angus Bridgeman."

"That's kind. As a favor, may I look at you closely? I'll explain. I am nearsighted. I can't see the shape of the moon, though people tell me it has one—well, no hurt there, I can design it to my own fancy. It was just good fortune I heard your voice when I turned into Harrow Street. Let me look at you clearly, yourself it is—do you mind?" His hands came lightly on Demetrios's shoulders, one grasping Brand's leash with one finger hooked in the loop. Brand too stared in uncompromised alertness, he who could love or hate in a second's flash. Demetrios felt Angus's clean breath inches away and saw a broad forehead knitting in close regard, Angus's own face open to study if the old man cared to search.

Though hardly scratched by experience, Angus's face held nothing amorphous or unfinished; the features were faultless, a healthy flush under clear skin. All the Bridgemans had big straight noses and prominent jaws; in Angus the look of severity was modified by a mouth that was tender and humorous. His hands were admirable with latent strength; dark red-brown hair fell heavy, shoulder-length, over the cream-white tunic. Demetrios did not remember seeing him before, with Steven Bridgeman—whose death, he recalled, had been shadowed by a hush-hush rumor of poisoning; but any death of a well-known aristocrat was likely to set up that kind of twittering in the Outer City. Angus must have been as beautiful at fifteen as now; perhaps it had been a day when Demetrios had felt sourly out of love with the crowd, wishing them gone as soon as he had begun to speak—yet he must have spoken well enough for Angus to remember it. "Let's be friends."

"So be it, Angus." Angus took his hands away.

"You will have been here when my uncle was murdered. Year Three—twenty-five whole years before I was born. Politics—it stinks."

"Year Three, yes. I wasn't in the market square when it happened. The community here that was looking to Simon Bridgeman for leadership—maybe a thousand of us all told, and many more still drifting in—we were badly demoralized by it. There had been, you know, all the hopeful dreams that human beings nourish after they've survived one more ghastly blunder. We were going to learn from experience at last, build a new world in the light of reason and justice, and so on; then the leader we like and admire is butchered in the public market by three ruffians with knives, and we don't know what to do. We didn't know, certainly couldn't prove, who hired the assassins, or if anyone did. Acting on their own, said Brian, who had been just an obscure associate of Simon's, his lawyer in fact, before the war. They were fanatics with a grudge, said Brian."

"There was a crowd, wasn't there?"

"Yes, a little crowd had gathered in the market to hear Simon speak and explain a new system of taxes. The murder was expertly done, Angus. Before the people really knew what had happened the men were out at the fringes and then gone into the woods. But you must know all this."

"Not too well. It's ancient like a passage in the histories,

like the martyrdom of Abraham that happened when I was
two years old. Well, maybe not quite. After all, my father
was there in the market and saw the knives. Your account
agrees with his. So nobody stopped them, they just ran
away."

"Yes, Angus."

"And that first Brian, who invented the label 'King's
Republic'—God, did he never look in a dictionary?—he
too died before I was born. Died promising the restoration
of the United States."

"He just might have used a dictionary. Brian I had
some intelligence, anyway shrewdness. One of those power-
drugged blowhards who say openly to their contemporaries:
'Look, you're all slobs and I'm another, so I'm going to get
mine.' Such fellows get credit for honesty and good nature
though they seldom have a trace of either. The old tiresome thing of excusing your smell by declaring everybody
stinks. It made a big part of the background for the 20th
Century cult of despair."

"Brian II has lasted. Dictator of the King's Republic all
my life." Like bat-wings at the edge of Demetrios's
thought moved the words: *Agent provocateur?* Demetrios
dismissed them, for good: this boy would not betray; to
think he might was itself a betrayal. "The wall between
Inner and Outer Cities was raised before I was born, too.
Till I was thirteen, everything beyond it was theory."

"Raised in Year Four, Angus. Brian I called it the reply
of law and order to the wicked, wicked assassination of
Simon Bridgeman."

"Aye-so? Building a wall against himself?"

"We don't actually know he hired the knife-men."

"Hm. The wall grows smaller. Demetrios, friend, for
these last months, since my family has allowed me to stroll
around in Outer City with no guard but Brand, I've been
feeling—oh, like a chick fresh out of the shell . . . Can I
talk to you like this? You don't seem frightened or—
well, cautious, the way most people are with me in the
Inner City. You're not currying favor, nor measuring out
the words you think would be good for me."

"We're friends."

"So be it, Demetrios." They walked on slowly together,

33

and Brand too was satisfied, following at the side as he was trained to do, with respect for human legs. "My uncle had no private police?"

"I think that's true. Simon Bridgeman, I recall, acted like a man who thought he was in no physical danger from those around him. Brian I—call him medieval, or maybe timeless; Machiavelli would have understood him. But your uncle Simon Bridgeman was very much a 20th Century man, Angus. A businessman before the collapse, which meant he knew all about making enemies, fighting with the dirty weapons of money and influence but never worrying about a knife in the gut, because that very seldom happened to 20th Century merchant princes unless they went into politics. A 20th Century rich man, and somewhat cultured too. He saw the disaster coming and persuaded his rich neighbors—some of them were real stinkers, by the way—to join forces with him in creating an enclave for survival. They dug into their mountain and renamed it Mount Everlasting—a poor choice I would say, for isn't it only natural that the hills should wear down and pass away like the rest of us?"

"Why was it Nuber you came to, back in Year One?"

"Judd Wilmot followed a rumor we heard after—after Aberedo. We heard a community here was successful, and accepting newcomers. The name confused us, because we'd also heard that Newburgh and other Hudson River towns had been demolished in the floods, especially one that followed a great earthquake somewhere north of Albany. We had seen for ourselves what the rains were doing—flooded highways, washed-out bridges, acres of muddy water seething—that's one reason why it took us from July into September just to go from Missouri to Pennsylvania. One day after Aberedo we met a little group like ourselves, only they happened to believe that everything had to be better in the *west!* Dear old Judd was remarkably angry with them, and they with us. Long live difference of opinion, and its cracking of skulls!—well, our quarrel with them wasn't all that fierce. They told us how the Mohawk and the Hudson had overwhelmed the banks from the Finger Lakes to the sea. What Lake Ontario was doing nobody knew. They explained that Nuber was a town fresh-built

34

around the nucleus of some Old-Time village and a fantastic underground shelter, several miles inland from the Old-Time city of Newburgh. Fresh-built by lunatics, they said, for God was about to destroy the entire northeastern United States. Wall Street was somehow involved in Jehovah's disturbed emotional condition." Angus smiled, not quite understanding. "The same prophecy was made during the return of Halley's comet in 1986—I was six years old then if you can imagine it."

"My father remembered the rains."

"The rains, yes. . . . Back in those ugly days others got wind of Nuber. We arrived here as part of a crowd converging from several directions. Your uncle dealt with us and found room for most, being stern only with the ones who weren't willing to work for the new city. With my hands, Angus, I helped to build Simon Bridgeman's tower on the summit of Mount Everlasting, and later, under the monarchy—excuse me, the King's Republic—I laid some of the stones that walled in (and protected) your childhood."

"And now I think you're helping me across the wall. Did you know that, Demetrios?"

"It's a function of old people occasionally. Sometimes their best reason for staying alive, though we do have others."

"I don't think of you as old."

"Old enough. . . . Well, your very intelligent uncle Simon Bridgeman probably knew the influx of refugees from chaos would soon stop—no wide communications any more, no large population left. Brian Gorman who took the name Brian I after the assassination—why, he seemed a nobody while Simon lived, a dry man, nothing remarkable about him but a heavy voice that told crass jokes, piffling echoes of remarks that had been salty and original when first delivered by Abraham Lincoln or W. C. Fields."

"What does it ever mean, calling someone a great man?"

"Maybe a great man is one who can stay out of tune with his times and nevertheless make himself heard—for good or evil: there can be evil great men as well as good ones; history offers full pictures of many of them, and has buried others in the compost of the footnotes."

"My head's running over with too much, Demetrios. I've begun to detest the artificial aristocracy I belong to. It's without basis—isn't it? Soon I suppose they'll be-calling us a nobility, with more flummery, pretense, arse-kissing."

"The centuries-old patterns shape up again."

"But meaningless, meaningless."

"Meanings unclear. You crave a meaning for life, Angus?"

"I've read the books—I know what America was, and might have been—yes, yes I do. How can anyone not want it?"

"We have to make our own meanings, not find them." The boy stared at him. "Evil-directed souls—the power-hungry, the cruel, the greedy and stupid—they have to make their own meanings too: even if they imagine that God or the Leader has provided them ready-made, there is still the act of consent, of agreement. And Utopias fall flat because they depend on the false notion that every person would want the imaginary good state if only he understood it—the hell he would: he wants his own dream-country, maybe one that includes slavery, and whips."

*Am I giving him too much, too fast?* The life of Angus in the Inner City, Demetrios reflected, must be like that of one caught in the quiet of the eye of a hurricane. Around him swirled the power politics of a little world still in a state of shock, old rules and new tangled together, nostalgia for an age of science still aching in a culture of ox-team, spade, bow and arrow. Demetrios had caught glimpses of Brian II on the King's rare pseudo-democratic appearances in Outer City, and had been reminded of a much-photographed Italian dictator of the middle 20th Century whose corpse, when the tide turned against him, had been strung up to a lamp post beside that of his mistress—almost a hundred years ago, yet here and there no doubt photographs still existed of that appropriate medieval obscenity. It has often been embarrassingly difficult to know what century one is inhabiting at any given time.

"Make our own meaning. . . . Demetrios, I ought not to keep you from home, but would you come to the Meadows awhile? That's a fairly good tavern at the edge of the park—might I buy you a couple of drinks? They

36

keep me filthy with more money than I can spend, even on women—I don't like buying sex anyhow. We could talk some more—sit out on the grass by Paddy's Place where nobody would eavesdrop."

"Demetrios never turned down a drink with a friend. I know Paddy well, and I've done my storytelling sometimes at the thing they call a temple, near there. Paddy would have been a highwayman in Old Time, or a used-car salesman."

They followed Harrow Street's climb into the parkland encircling the wall that Demetrios when young had helped to build. On the other side of the wall rose Inner City's terraces and graystone buildings to the rounded broad summit of Mount Everlasting. Good drinks they were, in the low long tavern building said to date from Old Time, and in Paddy's frog-face as he served them was a polite but obvious wonder, what old Demetrios would be up to with a white-clad Bridgeman. But Paddy was a genteel pirate whose single joke was to say that he avoided the common cold by keeping his snout out of other people's business. No crowd infested Paddy's lawn. Angus and Demetrios could nibble their cheese and drink the two-year-old Katskil wine in comfort, watching a slow-growing storm pattern enlarge over the hills. The park known as the Meadows was high enough to provide a glimpse, through a break in the mountains, of the waters of the Hudson Sea.

"Does your vision give you the meeting of sea and sky?"

"Without certainty, Demetrios. Light speaks to me."

Not far away, on a more tramped and weedy part of the Meadows, stood the Temple, which might have been well enough named had any god dwelt there—the wistful invitation of a name will not fetch them by itself any more. It was a wooden block of roof about fifty feet by twenty, on pillars of stone (people in Katskil have been heard to argue that the great earthquake north of Albany never happened) and its erection had been endowed by an Inner City philanthropist about ten years ago. He felt the People ought to have an agreeable meeting-place for like folk-dancing; he wanted it called the Mall, and it was to be like the Parthenon only some bigger, but when the money ran out he allowed it could be some smaller so long as it was rectangular. Which it was, but on the entablature there marched no frieze of splendor and strife—just shingles, which look neater and call for maybe less upkeep. In the 20th Century he could have hired experts to go to Athens and come up with a genuine replica, in Permagilt and wired for sound: to every century its own idiom.

Two groups had gathered at opposite ends of the shelter, one a flock of mostly young people, in solid-color tunic and skirt and loincloth—breathing flower-petals clustered around a center, which was a bearded goor in a red robe. The other group was of mixed ages and restless, crying amens, preached to by a harsh-voiced man in a gray loincloth. He had tossed his tunic aside. Repeatedly he placed his left hand on his ridgy ribs in the neighborhood of the heart, with thumb and forefinger circled, the other three fingers lifted, and his right hand spread out over the liver, more or less, indicating the carnal self—the sign of the Wheel and the Flesh. This was more and more commonly seen in Nuber, as the cult of Abraham grew. Some difficult people among the Abramites declared that the right hand ought to be curved over the genitals instead of the liver—makings of a possible religious war. The confused noise, as the two distant groups rather bitterly ignored each other in a spirit of love and forgiveness, reached Demetrios as mutter and squeak. Neither speaker was very good, the Abramite too hoarse, the goor too mellow. "Local Agora," said Angus.

"Ayah, but I believe Socrates was detained."

"I almost met that goor in the red wraparound, anyhow I think it's Goor Johnson. I can't make out his face, but there couldn't be two that fat, both in red monkeries. Senator Smith invited him to Inner City not long ago, a garden party, though I don't think the Senator's turned believer. Goor Johnson holds that the human spirit can't put off the shackles of the flesh and become one with the Unique Infinite unless it rejects the perverted doctrine of a spherical planet."

"Is there a nonunique Infinite?"

"Shee-it, man, forgot to ask. Anyhow the thing's flat,

okay? If we'd admit it we could ass-end to heaven right off, no sweat, Demetrios. Only sheer love for humankind keeps the goor earthbound—overweight has nothing to do with it. He made it sound attractive, but I was pervertedly munching maple-walnut cookies, and by the time I had them safely stowed some other sinner was crimping his transcendental ear, so I hitched up my shackled spirit and split."

"You're not ripe for heaven. The other noisemaker is Holman Shawn, preacher for the Society of Disciples, sometimes called Abramites."

"They're making converts in Inner City." Angus saddened at some thought that remained private. "Demetrios, has the proportion of freaks always been as high as it is at Nuber nowadays?"

"Oh, I think so. I dare say the proportions have always stayed about the same, maybe from ancient times—a handful of the very bright, a handful of subnormal and idiots, a multitude of the in-between, and everywhere a sprinkling of unpredictable weirdies like pepper in the stew." Demetrios brooded, bedeviled by a familiar distress. During the first years of his streetcorner activity he had occasionally told the story of the martyrdom of Abraham Brown, as his own sickened eyes had witnessed it—but not quite honestly. He had glossed over some of the savagery, the incorrigible human darkness, and might have made the poor brave fanatic Abraham appear more than life-size. Well, in a way he was, but so are all the thinking few. Crackpot or no, Abraham Brown did live with purity of motive and courage in action, and he did die for what he was, in the manner of Christ. Had Demetrios's tellings of the tale played a part in launching one more miserable messianic cult, which would infallibly pervert anything good in the man's teaching, and blow up all of it into whatever monstrous creation suited the fancies and the politics of the churchmakers? "Dear Angus," he said, "I wonder sometimes whether a life of quietism, or at least one of deliberate simplicity and very limited action, may not be the only one that does no serious harm. Even Goor Johnson may have a glimmering of that, if he isn't just in it for the money and cookies."

39

"The world stinks," said Angus. The boy's shift of mood caught Demetrios unprepared, as if Angus had tumbled into despair like one slipping off a narrow mountain trail. "It *stinks*. Not the world of course. Man. The dirty hairy animal—but damn it, he isn't always. He doesn't *have* to be—or does he? Cruelty, meanness, greed, sicknesses of mind and body, suspicion—Demetrios, I know a little about you. It's almost a fact that I came looking for you— no, I'd better say, I've watched for you, hoped to see you again ever since I first heard you, four years ago. I trust you, Demetrios. Do you know there's a stupid faction in Inner City that wants to make a politician of me? See themselves as kingmakers. Power stinks. O Demetrios, what am I to do? What is my work? The world doesn't want people like me."

"The world isn't capable of wanting. It just blunders on. I know—by 'world' you meant 'people at large.' Same answer. You will find your own art, Angus."

"How, in my ignorance? *How?*"

"I'd tell you if I could. Art of guidance? Leadership— teaching? I can tell you at least that things are unimportant. Love is never a thing, it's a country where we can make journeys."

"Demetrios, did you see Abraham die?"

"Yes. I can't believe martyrdom ever serves. It moves us but it doesn't teach. Our response to martyrdom is a self-indulgence. We remember the hemlock and the cross, but what have we ever done with the wisdom of Socrates or the compassion of Jesus?"

"Will you tell me the story of Abraham, though?"

"Yes. I must think about it. I'm tired now and disturbed."

"Forgive me, I've kept you from going home. Will you meet me here again? Tomorrow, near to noontime?"

"Tomorrow, near noon. Peace."

"Peace, Demetrios."

# CHAPTER FOUR

*Solitaire was Waiting*

*I never know the time on a day when I make a friend.*
                                    *—DEMETRIOS.*

Demetrios strode slowly down from the park toward that section of Outer City's fringe where Redcurtain Street occupies a slice of the arc, and perplexity traveled with him like a cloud of gnats. He was not what he had been before meeting Angus. In their talk neither had mentioned that policeman, but in Demetrios's loneliness the fellow loomed large. Angus, who would have grown up to regard an Outer City policeman as one more underling, probably thought the incident a trifle. Demetrios himself had simply forgotten Joe Park in the charm of Angus's presence. Past time had been clear before this hour just gone; now the present filled the horizon; yet Demetrios was not even certain that he loved the boy.

Angus belonged to modern society as old Demetrios of the 20th Century could not. *Three hours ago I did not know him. Faith moves no mountains except in the mind of the pious daydreamer; love is stronger, not compelled like faith to feed on illusion—it may do so, true, and thus poison itself, but it need not.*

He turned into a dismal alley, a short cut to Redcurtain Street. The houses here had been slung together of scrap lumber in the year before Simon Bridgeman's assassination, when refugees had begun to be less welcome in the city-state of Nuber; they stooped crazily toward each other like gossiping hags. Simon Bridgeman, son of the plastic age, never achieved a reliable sawmill. That was left for Brian I, who also understood the bow and arrow, pike,

41

and tomahawk. Nowadays they harness the streams flowing into the Hudson Sea and the enormous Delaware, and there's a quarry beyond Mount Orlook where they cut good millstones. In this alley Demetrios looked sharp for foraging hogs, scattered filth, pariah dogs vicious as weasels, and drunks. Not much violent crime plagued Nuber in the Year 47; what there was lurked spiderlike in crannies like this one.

He walked along briskly, swinging his walnut stick, keeping it visible in the late shadowed daylight. Sometimes the old man entered such places unnecessarily, recognizing the foolishness of it. One challenges the black spider to jump, and afterward feels—no, not younger, but perhaps more alive.

*—People still dwell in the wilderness regions beyond Katskil and other centers, exceedingly wild but hardly demonic as folk imagine. They live there from choice. They could abandon their feral ways and accept the shelter of the city-states—Katskil, Moha, Penn. But they don't. Now I am gone again.—*

Demetrios emerged safe from his alley onto Redcurtain Street, where the police permit nothing unpleasant. High powers of Inner City have always favored it, and own shares of course; white-tunic people enjoy the clean sidewalks at proper hours. Local custom requires the burial of garbage in the gardens behind the houses, so pigs and pi-dogs are not drawn to scavenge. Demetrios took pride in the flowers and vegetables he raised for Mam Estelle's establishment, although this came under Janitor Work only by liberal definition. Many houses on Redcurtain Street own bay windows and balconies where the girls sit on view, sharing these cosy promontories with sleeping cats. A charming street, at least in the Year 47.

On the front steps of Mam Estelle's, the Professor was musing alone with his lute when Demetrios reached home. He lifted a brown finger in greeting, missing never a note of the scale passage that flittered up and out of the heart's view like a climbing bluebird. "It's been a good day," said Demetrios.

The Professor nodded, spilling from the lute more diamond-dust of sound. Normally one asked him only yes-

or-no questions, since he was a mute. "A good warm day. I made a new friend, and maybe I'm happy." A glowing arpeggio acknowledged the possibility of happiness. The Professor's eyes were unfathomably soft, with gold lights. His skin was tan, his hair short and curly. Demetrios assumed his origins were partly black, but like many in the city-state of Nuber he admitted no past. They had been friends for years. Often the Professor, when the Mam did not need him in the Parlor, went forth into the city with Demetrios; his presence and his lute might lead the street-corner tales into fresh dimensions. This, and the sharing of Solitaire's bed, created bonds of kindness.

"The girls must be getting up by now." The Professor nodded, watching music fly away. He seldom smiled unless a south wind was blowing; today the wind was in the east. Momentarily Demetrios observed something of Garth in the Professor's luxuriant mouth, the tilt of his head, something of Solitaire in the long grace of his hands—not strange that those we love should share traits of appearance. "I never know the time on a day when I make a friend." The Professor found Time worth a respectful shrug. "Be with you again soon, paisan." In 47 this descendant of an Italian word had joined the other endearments of English, that Mississippi of languages. Demetrios squeezed the Professor's shoulder and entered Mam Estelle's sex-house.

The Mam was enjoying tea in the company of pretty Glorie and sallow Fran, casually using a squat pink tea set known to be genuine Woolworth, and lacing her own tea as if absentmindedly with fire from a jug of corn whiskey. As Babette crossly told her, had told her thirty times, she must have drunk enough Penn tea to float the Katskil navy—four catboats and a ketch. It was that time of afternoon when a protective haze so sheltered Mam Estelle that she let the house run itself, which meant that Babette ran it. "Mam, I declare to you, yourself it is, I got me this extra bicep just from lifting the durn kettle to the taypot for to make you tea and tea and tea." It wasn't the tea that worried goodhearted Babette.

"Take off thir'y pounds," said Mam Estelle gently, "and maybe your arm'll be thin enough I can see the bicep."

43

Blonde Glorie giggled; Fran's lips moved, likely checking some passage from the Book of Positions. Fran was a gentle, serious girl; to bed her was like earning academic credits.

Rugged Babette, maid-of-all-work here for the last ten years, usually got the worst of any argument. She greeted Demetrios with easy affection—they balled occasionally—and said: "She's through work, man Demetrios. Upstairs." Estelle sighed, busy perhaps in the corn-spirit haze with work-hours and the whole rusty, leaky affair of living.

A year ago Demetrios had found Solitaire wandering in the woods outside of town. She had been gang-raped, she said, and then had hidden and starved a few days. She could not remember who she was. He had brought her to the refuge of Mam Estelle's, as a special case. She could help mind the house, sharing room and bed only with him and the Professor. She was not to be touched by the customers, otherwise all three would split. "Needn't black-mail an old friend," said the Mam. "I'll love her myself."

Estelle relied on him. Who else would mind the fires and tend the garden for so small a wage, and entertain with stories in the Parlor apparently for the love of it? Where would she find the equal of the Professor, whose lute could give you the sound of children laughing or of breaking hearts? Mam Estelle had never been a pig for money, nor unkind. Soon she did feel and show a tenderness of her own for Solitaire—who even now remembered no identity for herself. Probably the girl's eccentric grace was being memorialized in the fat locked book, the Diary, which Demetrios recognized as a vital though slow-rhythmed heart at the core of Mam Estelle's existence. Mam Estelle was shyly proud of her Old-Time knack of reading and writing. No one else ever beheld the Diary: she had less vanity than most authors, and a better means of earning a living.

Solitaire was thin and sweet and small, and in a thin small sweet way she was quite mad.

Demetrios climbed the stairs and passed down the long upper hall, returning the lazy greetings of the girls who were getting ready for supper and a night's work, and reached the large pleasant room at the rear of the house that he shared with the Professor and Solitaire. From this

44

room one could look down on the garden and rejoice in its superiority to anything the neighbors had; also keep track of their affairs if so minded—sometimes he told Solitaire flyaway stories about them off the top of his head. She was sitting slumped on the big bed, dressed as he had expected in the slattern rags and stains of the day's work, her hair in a tight bun under a dustcloth, her cheeks smeared. The sag of dejection and premature age—that also was worn like a garment. It was horrifying to see her so, but Demetrios knew the compensations for this masquerade, this protective show that enabled her to go mouselike, unnoticed, about her labors. Sometimes she drew attention anyway, merely by a slimness and grace impossible to hide, but she was convincingly a drab slavey.

At this moment she was lost in gazing at that planet which endures and continues beyond all our windows. She turned her dark head slowly as Demetrios closed the door behind him, and in her brown eyes—droop-lidded they would have been during the day, night-fires hidden—her recognition bloomed: a bright fish blazes out of the murk of a pool in suddenness and gold.

"Solitaire was waiting for Demetrios." He had never known her to employ that upright pronoun against whose pillarlike rigidity most of us lean all day long and half the night; nor did she liberate the short thick blade of the other prodigious member of speech that rhymes with *who*. In the shelter of the third person Solitaire dwelt for her own reasons, and there she could be found if you loved her as Demetrios and the Professor loved her. "Solitaire has five hearts." She held up spread fingers. "One to keep, and one the dogs ate, and one for Jesus, and one for Professor, and one for Demetrios." But it would not be one of her bad nights.

"All mine. And it's been a good day," said Demetrios again. "Good and bad. I made a friend; but on the dark side, a policeman has told me I must get a license for storytelling."

"License? Phoo-ha!" She did not laugh; she was quick to see the possibilities of ugliness. Solitaire feared the dark, always wanting a low lamp or bit of candle burning even when she lay snug in bed between Demetrios and the

45

Professor. She remarked once that living was walking in the jungle, but sometimes there were friends. "Aye-so, and what will it cost, man Demetrios?"

"The cop wouldn't tell me, though I think he knew." Demetrios sank into the luxury of his armchair. Solitaire smiled. A certain ritual could not start till he was there, finished with the part of the day that took him from her. She never liked his going forth and squandering his stories on the crowds for their trifling money when he might have stayed safe at home. Once on a rainy day he had found her at a window blessing the clouds. But she never told Demetrios (or anyone) what to do. "I'll go to the Town Hall tomorrow and find out."

She made a silver yawny sound. A shake of her head dismissed the Town Hall and the whole blot of nonsense where tomorrow could scrabble after it. She pulled the dustcloth from her head and tossed it on the floor. She was bringing a light table and chair to the middle of the room when the Professor came in, and she smiled at him too.

The Professor pushed the door-bolt shut and sat cross-legged on the floor by Demetrios's armchair. His lute spoke as a part of his limber little body, soft-mannered and amorous.

Solitaire fetched her tinderbox (let no one else ever use or touch it, or she would rage and weep) and lit the candles in their sconces, placing them one at each end of the table. Then she brought, from a chest by the bed, a strip of red cloth, a pair of shears, a washcloth, a cake of soap, a basin, a hand-mirror. The basin she filled with water from the bedside pitcher.

Solitaire washed her face.

There must be a hundred ways of doing this—snorty-splash, flip-and-finish, grunt-and-slop, scrub-and-search, pinch-and-suffer. Solitaire just took the wet cloth and the delicate soap (for which Demetrios and the Professor paid high at a shop catering mostly to the white-tunic trade; but cost was barely comprehensible to Solitaire although she might dutifully ask about it; addition was a mystery, subtraction unknown, and money something that other people usually had) and removed the dirt from face and

46

hands. Most of it she had put there herself, part of the disguise. Though she worked hard and honestly for Mam Estelle, she practiced physical caution, mindful of her skin because her lovers desired it; and for its own sake too?— who knows? The Mam tried to limit her to such chores as bedmaking, sweeping, dusting, that would not expose her to soot and grease and stains, and Babette was usually on hand, ready to intervene with noisy competence if Solitaire needed help; for which reason Solitaire almost never wept or raged in their presence.

The hand-mirror was two-sided, an artifact of Old Time, and faultless; one side magnified, by a magic wholly marvelous to Solitaire. She loved the gadget because the Professor had found it for her, he could not say where. She brushed her black hair, crackle and spark and gleam, with another Old-Time treasure, a brush of true plastic, airy in design and flimsy-light. They are saying, Old Time will not come again.

She might have been alone, readying herself for an evening's entertainment or just observing her beauty as if one could do this with detachment. She loosened the slavey's smock to her hips and stroked each breast— round, bud-immature, warmly shadowed around the nipple —lifting it to the shine of the candles.

She cut a diamond-shaped segment from the red cloth, examining it tenderly as if it might be a creature of life, then slapped it down on the table and pierced it with a brutal thrust of the shears, so that the metal stood upright in the wood. Eyes squinted in pain, she spread her hands, letting them say: *That's how it was—if you care how it was.* Then quietly, a good housewife, moving about in nothing but her coarse linsey drawers, she rolled the table back to the side of the room, the shears yet standing. (Some time during the night—one of her good nights— she would slip out of bed alone and finish tidying up, putting away the shears, dropping the pierced cloth in the wastebasket.) She opened the clothes closet, hanging up her drawers and contemplating her wardrobe.

The Professor's lute remained silent until she chose from less than a dozen costumes a long belted robe of dull red with yellow trim and fine bone buttons of creamy white.

47

Demetrios and the Professor had pooled the earnings of more than a month to buy that for her. Of the other costumes only one was street wear, a suit of loose trousers and jacket, leaf-brown, that made her look, but for her way of walking, very like a boy. The lute exulted. One of her good nights, and time for love before supper.

She stood naked so that her lovers might know her with their eyes, her left arm underlining her breasts, her right hand out to warn that the time was not quite yet. Demetrios looked on the slender stem of legs widening to the amphora of hips, torso, midnight triangle, and to that sudden bloom of rose and darkness at the summit, her wise sad face. Reason dwelt there with her madness, and both were Solitaire.

The storm breeze was pushing at the open window. A motion of the Professor's hand offered to close it, but Solitaire shook her head. She slipped on the robe leaving it open, warm flesh shining. She said to Demetrios: "Solitaire is here."

He lifted her to the bed, and took her with the slowness and gentleness that were necessary. Over the house and the troubled city, beyond the homely jubilant toil of his body, he heard the desired rushing of wind and rain.

It was for Solitaire to choose which of her lovers would enter her, and when. For her the storm was so intense and shattering—certain revolting shadows gathering like wild hogs at the edge of a forest—that she could not bear it often. Demetrios thought of his body as a protecting frame for the central blaze. The Professor's lute murmured in tenderness and reassurance. Now and then during the long course of Demetrios's love, Solitaire reached out to touch the Professor's left arm, for when she did that (she said once) some of the force that guided his music through the strings flowed into her too and changed trouble to a singing.

She cried out in the extremity of the pleasure-agony, and lay at peace. In a while she said—for like the child that she was not, Solitaire loved a story all the more with frequent telling, and would be disturbed if changes occurred even in the small words: "Demetrios will tell the Professor and Solitaire the story of Anya the Goose Girl."

# CHAPTER FIVE

## She was Good as Gold

> Some geese will believe anything.
> —DEMETRIOS.

"Anya was a princess of Peranelios long ago, when magicians outranked even kings. Kings might lay taxes and order heads chopped off, but magicians could make people (including kings) vanish in an instant. Involuntary vanishing was felt to be unpleasant, although when the thing was done right the subject never came back to describe it: the Peraneliotic opinion was that we'd just rather *not* disappear zzzp! like that, leaving a small gray or dirty-lavender vacuum which fizzed slightly and then itself disappeared—phsssp! like that. Once in a great while a disappeared person did straggle back to Peranelios with some unacceptable tale of returning to consciousness in China or Brooklyn (we know there aren't any such places) and thumbing rides home. If these characters got tiresome about their problems, a magician was usually sent for to redisappear them.

"Magicians most often performed this trick—teleportation isn't quite the word—if they were asked some stupid question when they were trying to meditate.

"Anya was a good princess. As a little girl she never talked back, remembered to wash her hands, always pushed something better than the pope's nose to the edge of her golden plate for the deserving poor. She worked at being good. She studied her lessons, was kind to dolls and pets and servants, found out where babies come from by asking the cook instead of bothering Mama, and when the King was having a tantrum she said nothing but 'Yes, Daddy,'

49

and 'No, Daddy,' and 'Maybe, Daddy.' She was good as gold. Everyone thought what a glorious queen she would make, but she had three elder brothers, all healthy, so that was out: nothing to do but marry her off to somebody well-connected and not too wormy.

"As she grew from a little girl to an eligible princess, one thing troubled her. She liked being loved and admired —that's human—and one luminary at the court just wouldn't do it, the Dean of Magicians. He had a long cynical nose and was named Mennoc Moses, and by the way, nobody disappeared by Mennoc Moses ever came back. It preyed on Anya's mind. She thought of charming the old brute, but this would not have been sincere. You can't execute that kind of magician except by catching him asleep, which her father wouldn't consider; she couldn't do it herself because she was good. It preyed on her mind, right up to the day when the King told her he had arranged a luscious marriage for her with the Prince of Pommes de Terre. 'But, Daddy—'

" 'I see you mean to give me an argument,' said King Dagobert. (The current Prince of Pommes de Terre had massive gold and ivory teeth in the front of his face but none of his own; he was seventy-two, kept twelve concubines in stitches, and bet on the horses.)

" 'You know I never do that, Daddy,' said Princess Anya.

" 'That's right.' King Dagobert leered. 'You don't, do you?'

"Sadly she left him planning his takeover of Pommes de Terre, which has rich deposits of bezoar stone, and went straight to Mennoc Moses. 'My Daddy says I have to marry the Prince of Pommes de Terre.'

" 'Do you know,' said the Dean of Magicians, 'that you interrupted my calculation of the orbit of the comet Bolowje?'

" 'I'm sorry. My Daddy says I have to marry him.'

" 'Who, Bolowje? He died in 1846.'

" 'Pommes de Terre.'

" 'Oh, him. I wish you'd stop pestering. And you don't want to?'

" 'I'm in love with the cobbler's boy.'

" 'So go marry him.'

" 'My Daddy says I have to marry the Prince of Pommes de Terre.'

" 'Oh, *go* away!' As he spoke, the Dean of Magicians made an occult motion, inadvertent we feel sure, which sent Princess Anya whirling thousands of miles—zzzp! like that—and a thousand more, while Mennoc Moses scratched his shiny skull, watching a small lavender vacuum on the floor fizz out—phsssp! like that. What he had *meant* to say was 'Vanish, O Prince of Whatever-it-was!' He sighed, allowed himself one quick alembic, and went back to work.

"Princess Anya landed in Peraselene (*other* side of China) and the people of Peranelios lamented the loss of their dear princess, but not even King Dagobert felt up to tackling Mennoc Moses when he was busy. He was always busy. Dagobert rustled up a more marginal type princess for the Prince of Pommes de Terre, hoping it would blow over.

"And Anya? Well, she came down phlump in a grassy field in that country of Peraselene where everything is upside down only not very much, and the field had a lovely border of summer woods, and a charming pond full of white, brown, and brindle geese, who whopped out of the water, gathered around Princess Anya, and hissed. 'Stop hissing,' said Anya, 'or I'll tell your goose girl.'

" 'We don't have a goose girl,' said the Boss Gander. 'The last one quit. Couldn't stand the farmer's wife. Nor the farmer.'

" 'Then I'm your goose girl until we can make official arrangements, and I tell you to stop hissing. I take full responsibility, because I happen to be a princess by trade.'

" 'Is it all right if we graze?' asked the Boss Gander.

" 'Quite all right,' said Anya. 'Graze at will.'

"They were cheerfully grazing when the farmer's wife came to investigate. I forgot to say that the geese had honked as well as hissed, and that the good Princess Anya was wearing a fancy dirndl of cloth of gold or something, plus an attractive wraparound coronet which the Prime Minister had given her that very morning, for being good. But the farm wife was nearsighted as well as senile, and had forgotten her goose girl had quit. 'Where'd you steal the funny clothes?' she asked. 'Why can't you keep those beasts under control? Who do you think you are anyway?'

" 'This costume would occasion no adverse comment at my original residence,' said Princess Anya. 'The geese are quite well-behaved, asking only to be understood. In answer to your third question, I am Princess Anya of Peranelios, but I am prepared to act as your temporary goose girl, for the experience plus maintenance, until more appropriate arrangements can be activated. I expect to be in communication with Peranelios within a limited space of time.'

" 'What you are,' said the farmer's wife, 'is out of your head.' And she warmed the back of the good princess with a willow switch. She was a woman not much open to reason, and Princess Anya, after she was done crying, could think of nothing to do except be good.

"So it went on for some time, as they measure time in Paraselene, where the clocks are out of order as a result of being upside down but not very much. Anya had to rise before dawn, breakfast lightly on a crust of dry bread with butter on it, a tumbler of milk, and a pork chop, and go take care of her geese. That meant keeping off foxes and wolves, seeing that the goslings never got chilled, plucking the down—have you ever tried plucking a live goose? I haven't either—fighting off the farmer's boy who kept saying and saying he wanted to marry her, and generally making herself useful. In winter evenings when the geese were penned up she had to read to the farmer out of Gibbon's *Decline and Fall,* or Proust. He had begun both books when he was young; now that his eyes were failing he still hoped to finish at least one. It was a hard, grim life for little Anya, and often she felt the only friend she had was the Boss Gander, who loved to sit in the sun with her and hear tales of court life at Peranelios. Some geese will believe anything."

"Well, go on!" said Solitaire.

"Sure. Don't I always wait to be nudged at that point? Besides, I thought you were asleep. So we shall return to the court of Peranelios, where everything was getting sticky. The youngest of Anya's brothers had died of

52

measles, the second in age had turned priest, renouncing the throne in three languages, and what does the eldest son goodly Prince Cuthbert do but waddle off in full armor against the Visigoths, which was not only unprofitable but more dangerous than skiing and gave the cobbler's boy ideas.

"He was a nice kid—name was Hans. Princess Anya had met him only once, when she took her glass slippers to be half-soled, and they had sworn eternal devotion in some haste because she had to hurry off and dedicate a foundation. He was about to bring back the slippers—beautiful job, too—on the day she was disappeared. He swore implacable vengeance upon Mennoc Moses and then looked around for something more practical, but some years passed before the eldest son went to war and gave him at least the germ of an idea. He transmitted an offer to King Dagobert (through channels) to go find Princess Anya and secure the succession, in return for the usual consideration—half of the kingdom, and the princess. Dagobert turned him down flat.

"Word came fairly soon, however, that the Visigoths had (predictably) done in our national hero Prince Cuthbert—were in fact only a few miles from the gates of Peranelios. Dagobert reconsidered. Since Mennoc Moses was busy, he summoned Hans the Cobbler's Boy, apologized magnanimously for his hasty decision, and inquired if the offer was still open. 'It is, your ineffable Majesty,' said Hans, 'except I have to make it sixty-forty now—inflation.'

" 'Fifty-five forty-five?'

" 'Sixty-forty.'

" 'All *right* already. Some of my blood too? Convoy of pikemen and elephants? Travelers' checks?'

" 'No, your supernal Majesty,' said Hans, who rather fancied himself as a Galahad type, only practical. 'No, I mean to go alone, and simply. It will attract less attention. And—' here he really stuck his neck out—'and if I fail in my mission, do with me whatever you will.'

"Dagobert reflected that after all, nobody disappeared by Mennoc Moses ever had turned up. There was nothing to be done except get ready to make a deal with the

Visigoths; there never is. But he was a man who liked to hedge his bets when he could. 'Done,' said Dagobert, and he leered.

"Hans backed out of the Presence, and (as a part of his implacable vengeance) he hurried to Mennoc Moses with a proposition: ten percent of his sixty percent if Mennoc would just kindly undisappear the Princess right now. He knew—smart boy—that vanished princesses in fairy tales always reappear. But Mennoc Moses hooted at him. 'I could make the entire kingdom vanish if I was a-mind to, I should settle for ten percent of sixty percent? Forget it. Besides, I never undisappear anybody—matter of principle.' (The truth is he didn't know how.) 'But I'll tell you how to find her, free for nothing, which is what it's worth.'

" 'How, O fount of supramundane wisdom, if a Cobbler's Boy may so express himself?'

" 'Why, thank you, son. Oh, you travel east, west, north, and south at more or less the same time; then take a left, and a right, and go straight on for Peraselene—you can't miss it. Must get back on the job now. Nice meeting you.'

"Hans the Cobbler's Boy traveled off east, west, north, and south at more or less the same time, and took a left and a right, and didn't notice anything that looked like Peraselene, so he asked a redbird: 'Is this the way to Peraselene, your Eminence?' 'He's busy,' said the redbird —'I'm Mrs. Eminence. Well, you should have turned right back along there, but if you take a left by the schoolhouse you can't miss it.' And poor Hans had a number of similar experiences, until at length he encountered an Alien who didn't tell him he couldn't miss it—just told him where it was. All of which took time, time.

"Meanwhile back in Peranelios, King Dagobert had what may have been the first bright thought of his long and glorious reign. He asked Mennoc Moses (politely, when he wasn't too busy) to disappear the Visigoths. Which the old man did, with nothing worse than an irritated grumble —would have taken care of it sooner if he'd known that was what Dag wanted, and was there anything else on his mind?

"'O Lord no!' says King Dagobert, quitting while he was ahead. 'No, everything's fabulous. Have a good day.'

"And Hans, following the Alien's instructions, came at last to the charming cottage of Anya the Goose Girl, whom he recognized at once although she had grown up considerably. The farmer's wife had died of her own ill-nature, but the farmer still had hopes of getting through Gibbon, and Anya the Goose Girl was reading him page 2004 of Proust at the very moment Hans knocked on her door. She had less time for the reading now, with the housework and everything, but the farmer was patient, and still wanted to study the structure of each sentence. If dear Anya was a bit slow to recognize the Cobbler's Boy it was because her mind had to be on a lot of things; but then she recalled that he was connected with trade, and remembered more and more, and asked him: 'Did you bring the slippers?'

"'No, sorry, I forgot. But O my Beloved, half of my soul, I have come to take you back to Peranelios, and for this your noble father will give me half of his kingdom, or rather sixty percent.'

"'But I can't possibly—darling, give it back to Joe, it was his to begin with, you know that—sorry, I was talking to my youngest, he's going through a Phase—'

"'It's all right,' said the farmer's boy—'I got the little stinkers separated.' He had turned out well, by the way —I mean the farmer's boy—and tried hard to be a good husband.

"'Of course,' said Anya the Goose Girl, 'it was awfully nice of you to think of it, only you can see how it is.'

"'Happy to have you stay for dinner,' said the farmer's boy. 'Maybe go a mite slow on the O-my-Beloved bit, account we're sort of square around the edges, meaning no offense.'

"'And the felicity occasioned by his attendance at the prandial board,' said the farmer, 'would present no less an example of reciprocally desiderated enjoyment than a leisured appraisal of the summation he might elect to offer of his peregrinations—'

"'He goes on like that,' said Anya. 'Stay for dinner of course—Hans.' She did remember his name.

"So Hans stayed for dinner, and petted the children who were still of leg-climbing age, admired the squashes and petunias, and was introduced to the Boss Gander, who bit him, and headed back to Peranelios as soon as possible . . . Are you asleep?"

"Solitaire is not asleep," yawned Solitaire. "Because she knows there's more."

"And there at Peranelios Hans told King Dagobert the entire situation like an honest fellow, concluding: 'Therefore, your paramount Majesty, do with me whatever you will.' King Dagobert made him Chancellor of the Exchequer.

"Mennoc Moses—well, he drowned his troubles by marrying an astringent sorceress named Miss Givings, and they lived happily ever after, but the others in the story were a mite too young to do that. Are you asleep? . . .

"Are you asleep? . . . Mm, fair enough."

She would wake, to eat supper when he or the Professor brought it upstairs for the three of them. Then if the Professor's eyes besought her, she would give him the play-acting touch of the whip that was one of his needs, for it was a part of Solitaire's madness that she had learned a kindness toward what passes for madness in others. And she would then fall into the true sleep of night, from which she might rouse at midnight to put away those shears. Demetrios found it good to wait on her. Indeed a good life in most respects. What a pity—damn that policeman!—that anything should disturb it.

The image of Angus Bridgeman walked through his mind, beautiful and proud, gazing down from the summit of youth with curiosity and perhaps tenderness. Rain on the rooftop was lashed by a returning storm-wind that moved again toward quiet.

# CHAPTER SIX

*The Shards of a broken Mirror*

> *—and I to remember what never was, the Golden Age.*
> *—MAM ESTELLE, HER DIARY.*

Demetrios woke to the vermilion and gold of sunrise. Solitaire had risen in the night as usual to tidy the room, and would have sat a while by the window letting her thoughts reach after the storm-wrack when the stars came out. Now she slept in brown arms. The Professor would be approaching fifty, Solitaire nineteen or twenty; both looked like tender children.

Demetrios dressed in discreet silence and drifted down the stairs, refreshed. The giggles and squeals and running about of a work-night at Mam Estelle's, the occasional sob or slap or outcry, seldom disturbed his rest. He had not dreamed of Angus during the night hours: if the dreams of sleep would come to us at our command, who would ever wake?

In the large kitchen Mam Estelle was enjoying the early hours. An Old-Time aluminum kettle hummed on the iron top of the brick woodburner—stoves, some call them. In 47 not too many stoves could be found with those good cast-iron tops and easy-lifted lids; Mam Estelle had ordered hers from the notorious Salvage Company of Nupal, down the coast. "A good morning to you, man Demetrios!" The sage black cat was weaving and surging optimistically about Mam Estelle's ankles—cupboard love perhaps, but Jenny took it seriously as a fine art. "This is early time for you, a'n't it?"

"It is. Good morning to yourself, Stell."

Mam Estelle was never hazed in the mornings. While

the rest of the house would sleep till noon after the erotic tumult of the night, she and Jenny were up and had the world to themselves. Loveliest time of day, said Estelle: only time you can think. Her thought poured into her diary, a stream determining its own course.

Jenny was between litters, her spring output given away. Nuber thought highly of its cats. The big evil gray rats were no longer seen, driven out by the small dark-rufous ones, possibly mutants. The cats alone prevented the new breed from becoming a serious plague.

Dealing with the Salvage Company of Nupal gave Estelle no qualms. The charming kettle had come from there, the fine cast-iron skillets, most of the andirons in the bedroom fireplaces, and the noble two-level plant-stand in the sunroom that the customers never ceased to admire. In its rectangular upper section Mam Estelle grew pansies and marigolds; two tall healthy marawans spread up from the oval lower part. The stand was clear white without a flaw, a kind of porcelain nobody knows how to make nowadays. Demetrios and Estelle, having both grown up part-way in what folk still sometimes call the 20th Century, remembered the earlier function of these plant-stands—wistfully too, in the chill of the outhouse on winter mornings. Living in one century with a root-stub of memory in another, you must be mindful of the tender place where the graft is joined.

The Salvage Company sends its mule-wagons with well-armed crews to just about every part of the known world where decaying Old-Time roads or the dusty new ones can lead them, searching out any kind of junk or treasure the Company might sell for a profit. You hear stories about the collection crews stealing and watergating and so on. It's a dead-end trade of course, with that end in sight. In 47 the Company was thinking about starting a foundry, with charcoal from the Nupal forests and ore out of iron mines up north abandoned as unprofitable in Old Time; they also considered swallowing some of the small industries growing up in the town of Maplestock. Mostly scuttlebutt—but you never know about Nupal. Though included in the King's Republic by the treaty of Maplestock in Year 21, Nupal cherishes a persnickety half-independence, and is not about to give Nuber the time of day unless there's a dollar in it. "Town Hall," said Demetrios on his way to the outhouse—"Ech!"

"That license thing you spoke about?"

"Ayah, may the idiot who started it be enlightened with a dry cob. Is there paper out there?"

"I trust," said Estelle with dignity, but added more meekly: "Well, that paper we get from Maplestock is dreadful cheap stuff—it goes fast, and I did use some for —for writing. Notes, you know."

"Never mind, dear—in Old Time there was too much paper. We were choking on it, my father used to say."

"Sit you down, Dimmy," she said on his return. Jenny jumped into his lap and worked pointed toes. "I'll do you an egg."

"Bless you, if it a'n't too much trouble."

"Tsha-sha," said Mam Estelle, patting his arm. She was sixty-five—a young mother eighteen years old in a Connecticut factory town when the world fell apart. "License for storytelling! I don't know what way the world's drifting. Some time the Inner City people will go too far —snooping, interfering. And tax, tax, tax!" She broke the egg delicately into the pan. In her mornings Mam Estelle was inclined toward a soberly revolutionary outlook, too troublesome to maintain later during the crawling afternoons and evenings when she needed the consolations of the corn spirit.

"A nice brown egg," said Demetrios, "from Somerville's gang I expect. Obadiah's girls are coasting toward soup, Bab says." To Demetrios the chickens in the two backyard flocks, under supervision of the peppery red rooster Somerville and grave gray-barred Obadiah, were valued acquaintances, though Babette had the task of caring for them and permitted no interference. Demetrios minded the cow Julia.

Estelle was not so readily diverted. "Dimmy, I even wonder if it's safe to keep my diary. Some fella comes snooping, say it's a time when I don't feel too good, maybe have too much tea in me. Say he makes off with my locked book because some bloody new law says he can, and there's me indiscreet soul laid bare. For the vultures. No

59

respect for my gray hairs if they say it's subversion—now that's for to kiss my arse, truly! What's in Nuber worth subverting, hanh?"

"You a'n't gray," said Demetrios. "Lookit your pretty brown hair alongit my real gray. Bring your tea and sit down, Estelle. Tell me about your locked book, if you want to."

"Nay, Dimmy." She brought him his tea; stooped behind him to kiss the top of his head, clutching his long, badly combed thatch. But she had changed her mind about having more tea herself, and pottered about the kitchen with needless tidying—Babette kept everything in trim order. "Nay, oftentimes I think I want to talk about it, but some-way I never can. (You don't want out, Jenny.) It's just a book, a sort of—book. (Okay, so you want out.) And this is my time to go be with it." But she lingered in the doorway of her bedroom off the kitchen, troubled about Demetrios's day. Her room was originally a kitchen storeroom; she cherished it as a deer-mouse her nest, and no one except Babette was ever invited into it. Its one window faced east across the kitchen garden, and mornings came to her fresh and young.

"Don't apologize," said Demetrios. "I'll wash up my plate and stuff. You go be with your book."

She stood there a bit longer, sober-eyed, maybe longing to hear herself telling what stays beyond words—we keep trying. One subject is love, another is loneliness. No language exists for either except a few words and fewer lucky marriages of words that reflect bits of truth like shards of a broken mirror. "Well, don't get into trouble," she said, and closed her door.

The shortest way from Redcurtain Street to the Town Hall, the way Demetrios chose, takes you through Gallows Square, where you may see—you can't help seeing—the gallows, pillory, whipping-post. This is the same gallows that bore Abraham's wheel lashed to its crossbar so that he might hang in the public view as a warning to other enemies of the State. Some say it was not even intended he should die. The dreary tenements and shops surrounding Gallows Square also date from Abraham's time, squalid slattern buildings not redeemable by anything but the fire that is bound to take them sooner or later: what can Nuber's bucket brigade do when that heap of tinder and dry rot catches a spark? And some of the people who nowadays lean out the windows to study the particulars of a fresh whipping or hanging must have elbowed seventeen years ago for good places to watch Abraham on the wheel. Many would have died in the natural way of things —it isn't a good-humored world just now, so brawls would have accounted for some; others would have been taken by smallpox, cholera, yellow fever. Some may have just gone away, leaving room for newcomers who would observe another dying Abraham with the same uneasy excitement, and perhaps stone him.

Leaving Gallows Square you climb a couple of steep blocks and behold the Town Hall. Situated at the beginning of the pyramidal rise of Inner City, it is a fairly nasty hunk of architecture, a two-story blockhouse with a couple of fake pillars framing the door, the whole surmounted by a square bell-tower that would look excellent if it weren't twice too large for the building. It was built to accommodate a magnificent Old-Time bronze bell saved from the ruin of some church and dating back to the year uh-huh. The phony pillars rise the full two stories; if they were real instead of slabs of lath and plaster, they could really support the whacking great architrave that ain't there, but since they just cling to the building like bandages on a sore knee, there's room between them for a little piss-elegant porch called The Balcony, from which statesmen may address their public. The mess as a whole suggested to Demetrios a 19th Century style that must have been fading at the end of that lamented era, but left its mark, even in Missouri. What idiot revived it for the King's Republic in the Year 24 Post-Holocaust when the Town Hall was built, may never be known. Never mind—that damn bell-tower is *good*.

Squatting before its green, which is spacious, well kept, and rather pretty with the grass regularly scythed, the Town Hall is one of the four entrances through the wall, eight feet high, that completely encircles Inner City and Mount Everlasting. You go through the central corridor of the building and—if you have a pass or walk in the

61

company of a citizen of Inner City—step out on the lovely wide avenue that runs all the way around just inside the wall: it's called Wall Street. The wall itself makes a fringe around the base of the pyramid, approximately twelve miles in circumference. Nature built the pyramid out of the primal rock and men put the knobs on it. The wall angles up and down and all over the place as the flanks of the hills demand, but the pyramidal shape is always evident, reinforced by a triangular stone tower at the summit of Mount Everlasting. This was built to Simon Bridgeman's order because (he said) he wanted to watch the new world coming to him. It was the last of his brain's creations that he saw completed: he never moved into the sumptuous apartments high up in the fifty-foot tower, for he was murdered a week after the last brick was tamped into place, and Brian I, First Dictator of the King's Republic of Katskil (who liked simplified spelling because it saved time and was the only kind he knew) decreed that the tower should stand as an everlasting monument on Mount Everlasting, sacred to the memory of that great and good spirit Simon Bridgeman (deceased), savior of his people, prophet of the new world. Amen, the winds blow upon it, in 47 the tower apartments were occupied by Brian II, his queen and concubines, and Demetrios wasn't gosemplacing anywhere beyond the Town Tall.

He climbed the short rise to the green, only a little out of breath. Already the day had grown sultry, as though he brought with him a contagious sadness from Gallows Square. A few benches on the green were occupied by loafers; the police cleared them out at sundown and they drifted back in the quiet hours. A rag doll was lying on the grass—what sort of child would abandon a friend in that state? Demetrios gave it sanctuary on an empty bench, legs decently disposed. He saw a bland yellow bitch trot to the Town Hall, her hindquarters nudged by a zealous black cur who checked and mounted her on the front step while three lesser males attended; she looked patient and intent. A policeman came down the steps with a broom but only leaned on it. "Where do I go to see about a license?"

"What kind of license?"

"For storytelling."

"You must be nuts."

"I'm told it's required now."

"Oh—ayah. Second door on the right, ask the sergeant."

Demetrios walked between the pasted-on pillars into the acid urinary smell of small-town virtue. Entering that second door he found the human sludge of the night gathered to wait disposal. The only furnishings of the narrow room were two eight-foot benches, a desk flanked by an Old-Time brass spittoon, a heavy chair, a heavy sergeant to sit in it. At the far end was a closed door painted with the word LUTENENT. Waiting were three old drunks, one of them a palsied crone with bloodshot lower lids who might already be dwelling nearly beyond the reach of pain, a shabby fortyish man mumbling to his fingers and alert against eavesdroppers, and a weedy youth with appalled eyes perhaps still high on marawan. All of them made Demetrios think of patients waiting in a clinic—Dr. Justice is busy right now. The drunks would be put to soak in loneliness for a day or two, the jumpy mutterer might be anything, the youth would likely be turned loose with a warning unless his night's enterprises had involved serious personal injury or watergating. Demetrios had noted, over the years, how the city-state of Nuber was oddly lacking in civilization's usual chronic resentment of the young. So few of them nowadays!— maybe Old Time ought not to have considered them expendable like plastic dolls—cannon-fodder—vietnamable.

Now all five, plus Demetrios himself, must simply wait, until they knew every crack in the plaster of these walls, every dubious lump of shadow in the straw and sawdust on the stone floor. The nasty power to make people wait and wait is a built-in feature of all bureaucracies; whether the hazy autocrat at the summit is a monarch, an oligarchy, or a so-called sovereign people, the psychological smell of the waiting room is everywhere the same.

"I came to see about a license for storytelling—" maybe he should not have addressed the desk sergeant thus directly. The man went on writing. Demetrios had half-expected this routine discourtesy, stereotype of petty authority. It was irritating not to be able to read the sergeant's squiggles upside down: maybe the poor fellow was trying to finish a book. After more dippings in the inkwell his quill halted but was not laid aside.

"Who'd you say you are?"

"I am Demetrios. I'm told I need a license for storytelling."

To meet the sergeant's sullen gaze was to peer down a well at frog-eyes. He said at last: "Can't you find a place to sit down? You have to see the lieutenant—I got nothing to do with licenses."

"What lieutenant?"

"Like-man, we got only one on duty." As a concession to stupidity, the desk sergeant waved his pen at the door in the rear.

"When can I see Lieutenant Likeman?"

"Lieutenant Brome—oh, you think you're being funny?"

"No."

"Don't. Lieutenant Brome is busy. Wait your turn."

Demetrios sat by the worried youth. "Another warm day."

"No talking in here!" said the desk sergeant.

The boy inched away—*he* hadn't been talking, but what about guilt by association? Perhaps unseen Lieutenant Brome was eight feet tall. An hour oozed on into past time.

A single gray-paned window, where a black blowfly zizzed a bumbling prayer for more light, faced northward unacquainted with the sun. The swelling warmth of the day collected here nevertheless, squeezing forth antique smells to haunt the air. For a quarter-hour the weedy youth practiced rolling a marble along the back of his hand, catching it in the soiled cuff of his shirt, until the sergeant groaned: "Quit that, will you?" The nervous man mumbling at his fingers jumped as if slapped. A side-glance at Demetrios from the boy renewed their frail companionship in sin; behind his hand the kid amiably shaped immortal words: "Fuck 'em all!"

At last, the others disposed of, he was sent in to Lieutenant Brome and returned soon as Demetrios had expected, playing the legerdemain with his marble in plain sight. A sly wink for Demetrios and he was gone, whistling. The others had not returned this way: no doubt Lieutenant

Brome's office had darker exits. The desk sergeant sighed: "You can go in now."·

*Friday, July 19, 47.*

*D to the Town Hall dreadful early this Morning about the Bloody License Thing, please sweet God don't let him get Cross with them and rar up at them in his Pride that's going to get him into Trouble one day, he ought not to be plagued with that Shit and him getting on in years, and I to remember what never was, the Golden Age, when I lived at No. 2 Shannon Street with Sam and Steven and Leda, and there was Marcus my Baby. How it was, we said All of us was to be his parents and that was cool, why do I say it never was? Sam he is as plain to me now, his Red Hair and his Long Legs and his ugly nice Jaw you could hang your Hat on, plain as my wrinkled Hand holding this Pen, and there was always Marcus, Sam's Baby and Mine, though Stevie was always Best on the Mattress but never Loved me near so much—Marcus with Curls of yellow going thisoway and thatoway all over his Head like darling Half-Hoops of Gold only made out of Mist you would think when you touched them, that fine and soft they were, how could I write as if it all never was? Marcus he's dead but he lived, he lived to be Almost Three, I was fifteen when I Bore him, this I know, never mind, it was a Golden Age. And if Marcus lived they all lived, Sam and Leda and Steven, and we had this House at No. 2 Shannon Street cheap on account of near the Underpass and no Ground only a Postage-Stamp like of Front Yard. Most of the Bread, well, it come from Steven that had this Job at the Shoe Factory and just took the Shit like Day after Day so as we could have the Bread, and me and Sam and Leda we was on Welfare they called it, and there was People made like a Profession of it, I never liked that.*

*Sam he would have his Guitar, and Leda and me could sing, Steve said I was a Natural Alto. Oftentimes Abe Logan that had been Stevie's Lover and still was sort of, he would come stay a week or two, and he had a Recorder and knew a lot of Ancient Things that Steve knew too, see, they had been together on Radio once. Things called*

*Madrigles for an instance, and Sam could figure out Guitar
Parts for them, you never heard no Thing so pretty as
when we all got like turned on with the Madrigles. About
this reaching back, I tell myself Stell, you better not reach
back, you better not. Marcus he was Real-Crazy for the
Madrigles and would go Laughing and Dancing and Strut-
ting Around to the Music showing off his handsome little
Penis which he'd just lately discovered it, which Sam
wouldn't let the Doctor talk us into getting him Circum-
scribed, it was damn Foolishness Sam said, all they want is
the Dollars. Marcus—well-naturally Everything was a new
Discovery for my Marcus, you could say he grew up to
Three Years Old with Singing and Dancing. Oh it was hard
to wean him!—his Mouth was a Kiss of Red Honey and
the Sunshine Loved Him.*

Lieutenant Brome looked downright winsome in his ap-
parent desire to soothe and please. "Sorry you had to wait,
sir. That fool should have let me know you were here.
Demetrios, isn't it? Heard you once or twice. Pity about
this license thing, but the utopia has to be run on certain
principles, you understand I'm sure. Have a marawan
candy? I agree, too early in the day; sometimes I take one
though, strain of the job and so on. Doing much storytelling these days?" He leaned back at his desk, a bland
face inviting Demetrios into the company of the shrewd
who know how the world goes, a bit of yielding here, a
bit of sweetening there, no hurt feelings, everybody happy.
He was square and sallow, Lieutenant Brome, clean under
the fingernails but a little bloated in the belly, soggy in the
face, an athlete gone to slack.

"I was storytelling before 1993."

"Before when?—oh, that. We don't talk about that,
you know. Looking back is unutopian. Looking back, what
d'you find?—nothing but the outworn ideas, Demetrios:
democracy instead of utopian law and order, monarchy
instead of the utopian King's Republic, all that damned
socialistic permissiveness instead of utopian ethics, which
thank God the present administration is going to look out
for, lots better, from here on." Demetrios felt a new chill.
"Thank God," said the lieutenant earnestly, "we're begin-

ning to learn what it *means* to run things on strictly utopian principles! And get rid of any damned subversion
that shows its head." But after this fervent declaration of
politico-religious conviction, Lieutenant Brome again
relaxed, a reasonable, practical fellow, watching Demetrios
with the earnest, half-affectionate intentness of a fisher-
man who sees the float jerked downward by the dimly
seen victim. He went on presently: "Demetrios, I suppose
you understand how a government run on utopian principles can't very well put up with *random, unregulated*
storytelling, that could undermine the very foundations of
freedom and utopianism? Um . . . One great mistake they
made in Old Time—see, how do you think you're going
to protect freedom of speech if you let just anybody talk
the way he likes, umm?" *And the horror of it is, he does
not expect me to laugh, could not tolerate my laughter.
He has dried up the fountains of my laughter. Oh, if
universes are infinite, there is one where old Demetrios has
the courage to rise up, and hold off this manikin with
his walnut stick long enough to piss on all his neatly stacked
papers and wash them away down a stream of laughter.
And another where Brome himself can see the joke, and
piss off his own stream of laughter, wash the whole damned
world clean with laughter. But the devil of it is, that's
always some other universe, never the one we're stuck with,
where there's no such laughter, maybe none at all . . .* The
lieutenant had spoken some further words, so quietly, like
a murmured afterthought, that Demetrios was obliged to
ask him to repeat. "I said, Demetrios, the license costs only
twenty dollars."

"Twenty?"

"Twenty."

"Sir, that's annihilation. As janitor of the most respected
sex-house on Redcurtain Street, I earn four dollars a week
—generous pay but not princely. As storyteller with my
cap on the pavement, why, I can pick up maybe another
two dollars, if the weather's good and I go out five or six
days. My expenses come close to my income. I have no
savings worth mentioning."

"It's a shame," said the lieutenant. "If it was up to me
I'd allow for such difficulties." His face took on the inward-

listening glaze of one suddenly gifted by an original insight, a shining splendor for which he found suitable words: "See, I don't write the laws." The luminous nature of this presentment led him to even more exalted heights: "You can't make a utopia without breaking eggs. . . . Of course in some cases the inevitable, uh, hardships can be, we might say, minimized, in return for—I hardly know how to phrase it—"

"How much of what?"

"What?"

"What have I got that would make it worth your while to let me go on as I am, doing my job, telling my stories, and minding my own fucking business?"

"We're very direct this morning, aren't we?" said Lieutenant Brome, and giggled, tapping his fingers on the desk.

"Is it still morning?"

Lieutenant Brome stood up and stretched. He opened and closed the two doors of his office, glancing into the sergeant's office and a side corridor, apparently for listeners. "A man can't help it if he's kept busy," he said mildly. "It's about eleven o'clock." He returned to his desk, popping another candy in his mouth. "Just offhand—" nothing would ever be offhand with Brome—"how many other storytellers in Nuber belong to the Society of Disciples?"

The bell-tower hummed and roared and trembled to a music drumming down to the rock, eleven pulses of a Titan's heart. When he could be heard, Demetrios said: "Haven't the slightest damned idea."

"Come now, Demtrios. The more you fence with me the more of your valuable time I'll have to waste. You asked what you have that might be worth my while. Not much; but for certain kinds of information you might be, let us say, let off the hook—the legal hook, mind you. Mean to say, I'll tell you frankly and freely, Demetrios, I'm not altogether unimportant in Inner City."

"But I have almost no connection with the other storytellers." Demetrios struggled with disbelief, the stunned incredulity of one who supposed a drowsing tiger was soft because he looked so. "We are loners mostly. Artists can't organize, it isn't our nature."

The fingers tapped; uncharitable eyes gazed anywhere except at Demetrios's face. "The new statute gives me authority to inquire into the activities of, I quote: 'public storytellers and other persons of no occupation . . .' How long have you known Jon Seberling?"

"I never heard of him."

"Odd. He knows you." The fingers ceased tapping and wrote in a black book, the expensive kind bound in heavy paper covers that the factory over in Maplestock had begun to turn out in some quantity that year. "Mark Walton? . . . Edna McEloi?"

"I know of Walton, though I never met him. I've heard McEloi sing, and tell one very unpolitical fairytale to an audience that was mostly children . . . Lieutenant, may I say that storytelling is an occupation?"

"Indeed. But you are presently employed," stated the voice above the wiggling fingers, "as janitor in the Public Entertainment Facility registered under the name of 'Mam Estelle's'?"

"Of course."

"Of the customers at that Facility, what proportion are Inner City residents?"

"I haven't a notion."

"Indeed. Of the employees of that Facility, how many are members of the Society of Disciples?"

"None that I know of." But Fran was, and Babette had gone to one or two of the Disciples' secret Love-Feasts. *Do I get out of here in time to warn them?* The fingers worked on.

"The Mam Estelle Facility employs male prostitutes?"

"My recollection is that the term 'prostitute' was outlawed by the same statute that established the Facilities of Redcurtain Street. The Facility has had no male entertainers since that became illegal four years ago."

"Throughout history," the lieutenant recited above busy fingers, "the Crime Against Nature has been illegal, recognized as the Devil's own method of destroying Humanity by Race Suicide: this is Scientific Fact. It has therefore, naturally, never been legal in Nuber." Demetrios sat quiet.

69

The Public Entertainment Facilities dated back to the time of Simon Bridgeman who openly loved both women and boys. Brian I had not wished to disturb the Facilities, and so far Brian II's tinkering with the laws had been timid, aimed only at those least able to fight back. But Demetrios was being reminded that you don't argue with the rewriters of history. "By the way, Demetrios, is the Society of Disciples still renting out the use of its illicit hand-press?"

"Jasus, do they have one?"

The lieutenant sighed and put down his quill. Simulated geniality had vanished. "You spoke in your curious discourse of yesterday, on Harrow Street—which was reported to me in the public interest—of a hand-press. By the way, what's your last name? Can't seem to find it in my records, which isn't very nice for somebody."

"You amaze me. My last name is Freeman." The lieutenant wrote that down. "Yesterday, Lieutenant, I think I mentioned the existence of the hand-press in Inner City, known to everyone, which prints the journal *Hermes* and other legally permitted material. If I mentioned the possibility of another press somewhere, it was not from any personal knowledge of such a thing—I only passed on a rumor."

"Which can be dangerous and irresponsible. Well, between the years 33 and 43—correct me if I'm wrong—you were in the habit of publicly giving supposedly factual accounts of the death of Abraham Brown, of foreign origin, in Gallows Square of this city, in the year 30. This is correct?"

"I was in Gallows Square and saw him die. I told of it a few times during those ten years, yes, at the request of people who wished to hear it."

"But not, at least not in public, for the last four years?"

"Not in public nor in private."

"Why not?"

"I felt that interest in the story had become morbid, perhaps had always been so; that the actual truth was not welcome. Telling it therefore didn't seem to be in the public interest."

"And how do you come to be the judge of the public interest?"

"Every citizen is a judge of the public interest."

"Interesting," said the lieutenant, and wrote it down, murmuring the words under his breath. "Isn't it fair to assume, my dear Demetrios, that you have repeated the story *very* privately, say to your intimates, or—umm—or at the secret meetings of the Society of Disciples? Umm?"

"I am not a liar. I have never attended any of their meetings, if they hold any. I have not recited the story of Abraham's martyrdom to any audience since the year 43."

"Demetrios, you may go." The lieutenant's flat upward stare said without much equivocation: *Pray accept my gift of enough rope.* Demetrios rose, leaning on his walnut stick. "Nay, come back a moment, man Demetrios."

"You are not entitled to address me so."

"I stand corrected." The lieutenant smiled. "Demetrios, if by any chance you happen to tell again the story of Abraham Brown according to your lights, with or without the license we mentioned, it will be your misfortune. I consider this a fair warning. Understood?"

"Have a good day," said Demetrios, and turned his back on him. Perhaps the time was not remote when there would be a Brome dynasty, and it wouldn't do to turn your back. Demetrios walked out past the sergeant, into the newly cherished presence of the sun.

CHAPTER SEVEN

## The Prophet Abraham came from another Country

*But Jesus turning unto them said, Daughters of Jerusalem, weep not for me, but weep for yourselves and for your children.*

*—LUKE, 23; 28.*

The boy had said: "Will you meet me here again? Tomorrow, near to noontime?" So now to the Meadows, the lawn before Paddy's Place, from which one looked through a break in the hills to a meeting of sea and sky. *Am I late?*

Normal eyes could discover that horizon harmony; not the wide, nearsighted eyes of Angus Bridgeman. Such eyes, thought Demetrios, possessed a different way of seeing—his own were still 20-20, his knowledge of defective vision theoretical. *Am I late?* The 20th Century had automatically assumed "normal" vision to be "correct," the one and only, a characteristic half-truth. And how easily the old technology would have given Angus lenses! But lens-grinding was one of the taken-for-granted arts not provided for when Simon Bridgeman and his colleagues burrowed into the mountain. Normal vision would be a mighty convenience for Angus, increasing his share of safety in a world crawling with stealthy shadows—well, not many external shadows could be stealthy enough to evade the incorruptible eyes and nose of Brand—so yes, certainly, the kid ought to have glasses. Was not Leeuwenhoek, that distinguished friend of Vermeer, perfecting his wonderworking lenses far back there in the 17th Century? And with lenses, Angus would soon despise and forget the special vision of his myopia. . . . Was Vermeer nearsighted? —no answer; truth inaccessible under three hundred and seventy-five years of historical sludge, including forty-seven years of modern barbarism and another two hundred when nobody noticed that as a painter he was rather good.

But Angus couldn't have his lenses. *Am I late?* As he stood disconsolate on the lawn, a worm of pain stirred in the vague country of heart or stomach and crawled toward his gut where its transit apparently ended. He couldn't be late of course. The Town Hall had shivered to the eleventh hour of morning during his ordeal with the lieutenant less than an hour ago, and up here at the Meadows only half a mile away, he couldn't have failed to hear the prodigious bronze bell declaring noon. To worry about lateness was senile fuss. He leaned against one of the fine maples bordering the lawn. Over at the Temple a few idlers had gathered, Angus not among them.

At noon and midnight the entire city throbbed and ached to the full twelve strokes of that overwhelming voice. The knotty hands of the blind bell-ringer Blind Bailey would be guided to the rope by Little Reuben—Bailey needed no such guidance; it was simply one of their acts of love. For part of each night, folk said, Blind Bailey would sit cross-legged with the bell-rope at his shoulder, so that Little Reuben might sleep. Blind Bailey followed a clock in his brain as accurate as any mechanical marvel: to him the hours yielded their seconds and minutes with the patience of dripping icicles in the sun.

Folk said little enough about what would happen when Blind Bailey died—he was old; it might happen any minute—and the bell must be rung in some efficient, up-to-date manner by slobs like you and me. Some suggested Little Reuben could manage by himself, since he wasn't really a natural but merely a mite unsteady in his wits: it would make him happy, these theorists argued, to carry on Blind Bailey's work. Another school of thought replied, Not bloody likely.

*ONE*—The blow of the hour rolled to him over the rise of ground and some *TWO*—some white-clad shape simplified with distance crossed golden grass near the

73

Temple *THREE*—but no hound strode with that man; he showed not the shining grace of Angus *FOUR*—Angus in fellowship with daylight. . . . *Oh, he won't FIVE*—*won't come to me. He's forgotten, though he, himself it is, did speak of SIX*—*of meeting, almost as if he loved me. And what can I give that should SEVEN*—*should make him honor such a promise? Dry cakes of wisdom, no wine of EIGHT*—*of youth to sweeten them. The promise was made during a moment in the NINE*—*unexplored country of meeting. Can love be a trade? This I TEN*—*I take, this I give*—*what folly! Love is not any Thing, but love (if ELEVEN*—*love exists) must be that country where we go to meet*—*to meet*—*TWELVE*—*where we go to meet the only saving mercy*—

Demetrios walked toward the Temple, near enough to verify once more what his eyes knew quite well: Angus was not there. Demetrios would have found him at once, as your eye cannot evade the glory of a cardinal sudden in the leaves. Another worm of pain crept after the first into forgetfulness. What he needed was a good sneeze, a cough, a roll in the hay. What he needed was a goddamn drink.

He entered Paddy's Place, scanning the cool retreat, the bar, the little booths, open tables on the floor's fresh sawdust, instantly recording the already known sadness: *Angus isn't here.* Paddy, wiping the bar, observed him with politely silent curiosity, his smile a modest widening of the frog mouth—you expected it to open at sight of a penny-insect with the zip of a lightning tongue.

A pair of nondescript men, travelers likely, overnight guests, were eating lunch or late breakfast in a booth, where they chewed some private topic in undertones. Paddy's Place was a prosperous hostel near enough to King Brian's Wall to catch trade from Inner and Outer Cities, and connected by a long decent street to the Great South Road, which comes from somewhere in the north, passes through Maplestock and Kingstone touching Nuber at the fringe and proceeding south through Nupal and through wilderness as far as Sofran. There it bears west, avoiding the areas of poison desolation, and so reaches Penn, which is a republic but not a King's Republic. The only other customer was an old fellow beginning a profound soak in Paddy's beer. "A good day, Paddy," Demetrios said; his foot found the comfort of the rail. "If you know something good about it."

"Why, the sun do shine, man Demetrios—I mean it would if I'd persuade me new slut to wash the windies, and what'll it be?"

"Shines from force of habit, man Paddy, like the joe who kept grinning when they cut his head off, so as not to forget what the joke was. Corn spirit, Pad, I do need a touch of the corn spirit."

Paddy reached for the jug. "Dark blue today, yourself it is. The way I heard it, he couldn't tell 'em the joke because he was short of breath. Things look nice after the rain."

"The pee of Zeus. The floods of Old Time at Aberedo."

"Ayah." Paddy resumed his day-long wiping of the bar. "Aberedo?"

"A town in Penn, where I stopped once." Demetrios drank, pushing his coin about in a puddle from the bottom of the glass. "Maybe you was never there."

"Nor heard of it."

"Refill, dear soul. I'll drink slow, trouble you no more."

"No trouble, sir."

"Sirring me, you Irish monster? Why, old Quixote's armor is scattering rust like red dandruff. Time, mind you, is not the only cause of it: the fella was born old." The (other) old drinker was deep-sunk in his beer dream. Older than Demetrios, he too would have been born in the age of plastic and subsidized corruption: maybe the dragons, magicians, imperiled beauties of his fantasy were powered by internal combustion, wore white lab coats and garments by Saks Fifth Avenue. The travelers, done with their conference, sat heavy with digestion, picking their teeth with splinters—why, by nightfall, if they had good horses, they could be twenty or thirty miles from Nuber—

*So, Demetrios? You could have wandered away from Nuber any time in the last forty-odd years, but always found some reason why not—maybe sprouting from a delusion that there's really no world beyond it. To leave it is*

75

to enter a mist. But there were substantial reasons. There was Elizabeth of Hartford, sweet none-too-bright Elizabeth who was like a wife or better for eight years after George and Laura moved away, until she died giving birth to the big-skulled mue which also, by one of the occasional mercies of nature, could not live. There was the Orgy Decade, the Twenties, my thirties, aftermath of the Red Plague when nearly everyone in Nuber believed the end of the human race was at hand—but this time really-truly, as it always has been of course—and so one might as well try and try for some new way of touching off an explosion in the genitals, calling this action Life as if other happenings were something less than Life. But the nervous system can shudder only just so much, so what else is going? Why, to us in the Year 30 the prophet Abraham came from another country, Abraham who believed like other holy men of other ancient times, that something he called the love of something he called God was bigger than either the dollar or the orgasm. I don't know. You can't spend an abstraction to buy you bread. You can't love an abstraction, but only other individual human persons—love directed elsewhere ceases to deserve the name, and may become poison or nonsense, or perhaps a kind of mental masturbation that can't come. Anyhow they butchered him.

Why could you not be here, Angus? Your nearness alone might almost content me, even if you never desired to touch me. But your absence is a thorn in the heart that teaches me I love you.

The prophet Abraham came from another country—

Demetrios pushed coin and empty glass away, and let his walnut stick thump the sawdust as he made for the door. He nodded to those travelers, who lifted their mugs amiably, guessing perhaps that Demetrios understood country roads and open skies. "Have a good day, all," he said, and stepped into a wave of sunlight, which transfigured the Temple and its shingled entablature so that it did seem a fantasy-glimpse of the Parthenon in the shade of Mount Everlasting.

He strode down to it, his eye (professional though a mite drunk) assessing the crowd. Mostly young or youngish; no babies prepared to let fly with howls in the midst of dramatic passages. Another white-clad man was coming down the avenue that curved from the southeast gate of Inner City, the route that Angus would probably use. But it wasn't Angus. Just another stranger who, as Demetrios halted to observe, unobtrusively spoke to the handful of others in the crowd who wore the white tunics. And then by ones and twos, with too much unconcern, they were drifting back up the avenue to that southeast gate, the careful messenger being the last to depart. *Something is happening in the Inner City. Where Angus lives. News will trickle down to us in time, whatever we are allowed to know.*

Smoldering grief at the boy's absence, smoldering wrath at Lieutenant Brome, at the law which is an ass, mixed with the corn spirit and the morose sultriness of July. A few eyes in the placid crowd were already asking: Will the old boy give us a tale?

He rested his back against a pillar of the Temple, his bones familiar with every bump of the bricks. Two weeks ago he had lounged here giving them Hans Andersen's *Little Mermaid* as it came through the lens of his memory. *"Demetrios, if by any chance you happen to tell again the story of Abraham Brown according to your lights—"* he dropped his cap upside-down at his feet—*"with or without that license we mentioned—"*

"Hear me who speak to you: I tell how the prophet Abraham came from another country.

"He was born, dear souls, in a town named Bethel in the state of Maryland. This was in 1988, five years before the Destruction. Of Bethel he remembered only the name and random childhood images, for his family moved to Ohio and he was there, a child of five, when one of the bombs removed the city of Washington from history. These things he told me in a quiet conversation, the day before he was betrayed.

"Abraham was not hard to talk to. We chatted comfortably, as might any two men with a few common interests. He did not condemn my agnosticism though his mind would not allow him to understand it. He was a man of middling height, with reddish beard and sandy hair worn shoulder-length. Blue-eyed he was, simple of

77

speech, and it seemed to me most of his followers had acquired traces of his simplicity. They were a little army of fifty saints, the majority of them children. Painted on their white tunics they displayed the symbol of a wheel crossed out by two strokes, to express their belief that God had declared against all mechanism. No more machinery, said Abraham, who felt that God spoke through him. No more use of meat, leather, milk, eggs, no more subjection or destruction of other living beings. The idea is older than Buddha and newer than tomorrow. If people must travel, Abraham said, let them walk, as these children had walked with him into the northern wilderness and then south to Nuber. He also proposed to transform Nuber into the New Jerusalem.

"I met that band of the faithful in the orchard of one Cecil Mason, since deceased, who had allowed them the use of it for a campsite after they were admitted through the border posts into Outer City. The orchard is still maintained by the son of Cecil: you can be shown the spot where Abraham's tent was raised. That is the spot where the disciple Jude brought the police of Nuber, and in their presence accused the prophet of planning the overthrow of the state. I had talked a little with Jude also, that day in the orchard. He was then a man inwardly ravaged, though I did not then understand the cause—nor do I now. But I think he acted, not as some say out of greed for tainted money, but from a desire to arrest the world's attention, even its compassion, by acting the part of the chief of sinners: to become the most hated scapegoat, to take on the load of sin by sinning to the uttermost, to reject the wine of life and choke to death on a mouthful of ordure, as a way of saying: 'Behold, O Lord, what I have done for Thee!'

"I spoke too with the disciple Mathias of Gran Gor, who believed Abraham had healed him of the smallpox by a laying on of hands, and believed also that Abraham was the second incarnation of Jesus Christ, only begotten son of God, returned after two thousand years to save the world. Mathias was even then contemplating the task of writing down the story of Abraham's life on earth. He may be engaged in this now: he left Nuber after the martyrdom and I don't know what became of him, nor whether he believes the world has been saved.

"Abraham earned his living as a carpenter up to the twenty-eighth year of his life. This was in some fairly large settlement of survivors in Ohio; he never told me the name of it. He said those were years when his enlightenment strove with his folly, until at length it was clear to him that God and the Devil were battling for his soul. Then into the wilderness went Abraham alone and naked by God's command, and wove himself garments of grass, sandals of grass with soles of wood carved by the knife that was his only tool and that had never drawn blood. In a clearing of the forest he made a shelter and a garden sufficient for his needs. I have heard the fairy tale about the fox who guided him to edible plants and berries and mushrooms, but Preacher Abraham himself told me no such nonsense. He knew and loved animals too much to falsify them, and because he was quiet, slow-moving, harmless, they came to him. I was not surprised that he knew the legend of St. Francis of Assisi and called St. Francis 'my brother'—and to me at least he never made any claim of supernatural origin. I think his one concern was to tell people how he thought they might live so as to be at peace with themselves and pleasing to the God in whom he believed. . . . He lived three years in that shelter in the forest, and was joined by the disciple whose name was John, by another who took the name of Simon, and in the third year, by Jude."

—*And I must elbow some room away from Demetrios for my Mam Estelle, and also comment that there's more than one way to skin the ecology. The most learned definition I can find for the word "impractical" is "of or pertaining to whatever won't work because we can't be bothered." It would be practical to live by Abraham's principles, though maybe tedious, if we were mostly Abrahams instead of protein-hungry, rumpleheaded sexpots like you and me and little Cousin Jasper who, when too young to be quoted, did manfully enjoy himself behind the barn with that precocious Lily Littlejohn from down the road. It wasn't just sex either—Jas had ripped off a hunk of mince pie which they divided, and that little fiend Lily*

79

*had liberated a far-out pair of turkey drumsticks. Domesticity yet. Now Estelle.*

[*More of Friday, July 19*]

He's late, but remembered to milk Julia before he left, Babette said. I won't have no more Tea till I hear Solitaire come down to do the kitchen. I want to start turning this Book into the Story of my Life, not just a Diary. If you write each Day that is like only looking out the Window, but the other thing, the Life Story, that is going up on a Knoll like the one back of our House in Raeburn by the Underpass, well, it had been a piece of a Park once, I remember that busted Bench, and up high there you could look for miles.

So when the House by the Underpass was knocked flat by what they said was Blast from what happened in New York City Forty-Five Miles away, I was down Cellar looking up a pint of Peach Pserve. I made it myself, they All liked it. I was caught by half the Floor falling in onto me, one of the timbers pinned my Leg so it took me an Hour or two to fight my Way loose. I knowed the leg was not broke, but something was holding up the Timber a Couplethree inches, but I couldn't get free till I was able to tear loose a Stick that had splintered off of Something, and pry up the Timber a bit so as I could inch out. There was Cobwebs all over the Timber, that gray stuff mixing with the Blood off of my Fingers where I had Some Trouble with the Stick, and a nail stuck out of that damn timber down into my Leg, tearing deeper into the Calf whiles I was fighting Loose, and all that time I could hear the Sireens howling and people yelling but like Way Off, and once I guess it was a Fire Truck went by, much good that would do, but in our House nothing at All, and still I knew, Jesus God, they were all there, they had to be There, Stevie and Sam and Leda, and I kept asking, Jesus God, why isn't my Marcus crying, why isn't He? There wasn't anything I could of used to cut my foot off, I had to keep prying with that fucking stick, and so when I did get loose in an hour, two Hours, Whatever, I swear I must of picked up that Pint of Peach Pserve off the Cellar Floor, because I had it in my hand when I scram-

*bled up the wreck of the Stairs and found out what had Happened, how it was. I don't know where I flang the goddam thing. There was the teevy, see, knocked clear across the room, it only hit the back of his head, Marcus his Face was not hurt at all, Sam's throat was cut with the flying glass, you couldn't see how anything had happened to Stevie and Leda but they was both so quiet Dead, it must of been the Blast. I carried Marcus to the top of that Knoll, his Face it was not hurt at all, and I never did know before the long Way you could see from that Knoll, I sat there with my Leg bleeding into a funny red Puddle, Jesus God you could see for miles and miles.*

*So later when I was working at this House which was Mister Fleur's Establishment in those days till he died and left it to me, why, Men would ask me about the long Scar on my Leg. I never told them, never told Anybody except Babette which is like talking to the Pulse in my own Heart. Might be I ought not to try to write about the Past Things that Happened, but some-way it's like on me to do it, because that type World isn't ever coming back, and maybe People ought to know—now look at me Imagining anybody will ever read This!—I think they ought to know how it wasn't All Good.*


"At the close of those three years Abraham set forth with his disciples to preach the life of simplicity. One would think that in the aftermath of 1993 human beings should have been ready for it. It did not prove so. A generation had passed—thirty years including the time of the Red Plague. Men and women in their twenties had no personal recollection of the world as it had been, and small faith in their shattered elders' talk about it. People, old and young, wished to live—why, more or less as people always have done: blundering, credulous, self-obsessed; half-educated monkeys with scant thought for the morrow and none for the past. (Aren't we like that, dear souls?—it's hard, tiring work being any more human than that.) When Abraham preached, most listeners stared, muttered, walked away. A few exceptions became loyal followers.

"Abraham found most of his listeners were children.

81

If he asked himself why, he gave himself only the truistic answers—they were innocent, open-minded, and so on.

"He traveled north through Penn into the nation we now call Moha, and crossed the Hudson Sea with his company on makeshift rafts—there was no reliable ferry in those days south of Ticonderoga—into what we once called New England. He won many more followers there. Everywhere in that land, he told me, he found small communities holding together, some declining, but a few almost prospering in the ancient manner of self-reliance so emotionally despised by self-adoring intellectuals in the sad latter days of Old Time. But the children who slipped away from their families to join him, often following secretly through the woods until they were too far from home to be sent back, were not all recruited from the bored and discontented; many had the true flush of faith —I saw it myself. Abraham soon gave up trying to send the children home, and accepted their devotion as a manifestation of God's will. They came to be called Abraham's Army, or the Roving Ragamuffins, or the Children's Crusade. Weak small settlements feared their approach because they had to eat. They were never thieving, nor disorderly, nor violent. Before the troubles they encountered on Adirondack Island and south of there, they numbered over two hundred.

"The disciple Andrew remained behind in Moha to find a site for the New Jerusalem. There was good country available everywhere, going back to wilderness; but when Andrew rejoined Abraham in the north he also described the city of Nuber, and the prophet turned south with our city for his goal—guided, he told me, by God's voice in a dream.

"He came in the fall of the year, close on the day we celebrate as the Day of Forthcoming, that day when Simon Bridgeman's people left their refuge in the mountain and learned the earth had not been altogether destroyed. Nuber, unlike other towns, had prepared itself with fear and resentment against Abraham's appearance. One Cephas in particular, who was Master of the Carpenters' Guild, had alarmed the people with accounts of Abraham's preaching; and he had found an ancient oaken wagon wheel, and declared that Abraham ought to swing from it in Gallows Square, for threatening to upset the utopia. 'He has crossed out the wheel over his heart,' said Cephas—'let him take it on his back, and let us see if it will roll him into the New Jerusalem.'

"Abraham's legend had grown, dear souls. His horde of hungry children—they were only fifty, after an encounter with smallpox at Gran Gor—was dreaded like a plague of grasshoppers; but that's no full explanation of what happened. Why was Christ hated, who harmed no one? Why do we demand his crucifixion again, and again? Can it be, dear souls, because he said, *Love thy neighbor*—? Pilate found no fault in Jesus, but yielded to the clamor and gave him to the mob. Abraham, true, was officially sentenced by the magistrate at the Town Hall, to one hour of public discipline as an enemy of the State; yet Judge Bruecke says to this day that he had no thought of condemning Abraham to death. He intended the fellow should spend an hour in the pillory, no more—and even that, he says, was simply in order to quiet the public unrest.

"Oh, let folk argue it as they argue the thoughts of Pilate, or the thoughts of the archons of Athens. The disciple Jude did bring the officers of the police to the orchard, and stood outside Abraham's tent and called to him. And when Abraham came out Jude kissed his forehead saying, 'O my Master!' Then the sergeant of police asked: 'Is this the man who declares the city must be destroyed so that another may be built?' Jude said, 'It is he.'"

Demetrios saw new faces at the Temple, a few. More stragglers were crossing the grass of the Meadows, among them two men in the uniform of the police. Some distance away, but advancing more quickly when he noticed the crowd, a boy or young man in a green shirt. Not Angus, too heavy-set. Garth? Garth ought to be working at the stable. Maybe he had a long noon hour. It was Garth. *Warn him somehow.*

"And they took Abraham before the magistrate, who questioned him—speaking reasonably, I'm told, even going so far as to explain to Abraham why the State found it

83

necessary to chastise him if he would not admit himself in error. Abraham stood silent.

"And when he was being taken from the Town Hall a crowd led by Cephas seized him from the police, overwhelming them, and lashed his arms to that wheel which they had decked with garlands of briers, and made him carry it to Gallows Square. This I saw, dear souls, with my own eyes, and I saw Judge Bruecke come out on the balcony of the Town Hall and call down to the mob: 'There must be no disorder, no disorder!' A few others beside myself were able to hear him.

"Abraham carried his burden to Gallows Square. There were at this time two malefactors in the pillory, one a thief, the other an unlicensed beggar. Therefore the mob lifted the wheel to the crossbar of the gallows, that Abraham might hang there; and they stoned him. The beggar called to him from the pillory: 'Lord, remember me!' But if Abraham replied the sound was broken by a stone.

"I spoke with a Christian in Gallows Square, who reminded me of a verse in the Gospel of Matthew: *But all this was done, that the scriptures of the prophets might be fulfilled. Then all the disciples forsook him, and fled.* I asked him, How often, how often must Christ be crucified? He was only grieved by my question and left me without responding.

"In the first hour of evening, Abraham cried out: 'Where is the New Jerusalem?' I heard one voice answer him out of the dark of the crowd: 'Not here, O my dear Lord, not here!'

"At some time during that hour Abraham died."

# CHAPTER EIGHT

## The Happenest Day of My Life

*Many heroes lived before Agamemnon, but all are submerged in the long night unwept, unknown, because they lacked a sacred poet.*
*—Horace, ODES, IV; 9.*

The two in dark uniforms approached casually—no disturbance wanted—a few yards behind Garth's innocent grin; the boy had not caught on. Demetrios let his walnut stick tumble at Garth's feet, and stooped for it as Garth did—he would of course, bless him! When their heads were close Demetrios mumbled: "Keep clear so you can help—lose yourself in the crowd, fast!" A moment of shock, and Garth understood; he became a blue-eyed fox peering through the bush of a fat woman's frizzed-out hair ten feet away.

"Got a license?" They were officers Demetrios did not know; but they knew him. *What have I done? What can I prove except my own stupid anger? O Solitaire!—*

He should have thought of her before. "License?"

"Come on," said the beefy one. "You can explain it to Brome."

"Cossack!" shouted the woman with frizzy hair. "He didn't do nothing only talk about holy Abraham."

"Just keep back, folks. Mind your own business." She did, like the rest of the gazing crowd; the lean one secured Demetrios's arm, his hands heavy with uneasiness.

"Why, I'm coming quietly. Mind my stick there, it's a palindrome. Lose that or mishandle it and you'll be the sickest man alive."

"A what?"

85

"Palindrome. At least carry it upside down, man, so the power won't flow into your arse crossways."

"Maybe he—uh—better carry it, Cass? If it's one of them what he said?"

"Well, I guess not," said beefy Cass; but on the long walk down across the Meadows to the town lockup, Cass held the stick at arm's length, and upside down so far as he could without quite knowing which end was the top.

"Aren't we going to the Town Hall?"

"Brome is busy, Mister," said Cass. Demetrios saw the pursed smile of a bully not quite sure of his powers. "Put up with our hospitality a while, Mister." The lean one's hands now held no more than a token grip. "Be our guest, Mister," said Cass.

The lockup was a one-story lump of mortared stone at the end of an alley from which a path straggled up into the Meadows. Oak trees spread green sadness over lesser growth by the little jail, over its yard with one bench, one upright post. Rings on the post served for hitching horses, or people. No other building stood in sight. No sunshine, no breeze—yes, there was a breeze, a whish-hush of the upper leaves underlining silence. Daylight, but to Demetrios's mind came the taste of perpetual evening.

The one-eyed stubble-faced jailor, his bundle of keys too large for him, gazed up at Demetrios with the distrustful pleasure the man with the club might show before a haltered bull. "Cass, what've you brung me? This ain't no lazy idle beggar. What you done for your country, Mister? Been into the till? Raped some little twist? Kind of forgot your old self in public? Hey?"

"Put him in the tight one," said Cass, "and keep your thoughts inside your brains, Putney. No fraternizing. Brome says."

"I have news for you, Mister Cass. We may appeah to live a retired life heah, but all my three apartments is full, Mister Cass, and what do you think of that?"

"Put him in with Bosco then, it'll make a pair of 'em. But no fraternizing with this'n. Oh, and keep this someplace." Cass set the stick respectfully in a corner of the room that served Putney as reception hall, office, kitchen, bedroom; a chamber pot stood out from under the bed

86

doubling as spittoon. The inner door gave on a corridor serving the three cells; Putney liked to keep it closed, enjoying his privacy and his own flavors.

Demetrios was relieved of his tinderbox and the few coins he had salvaged from his cap. Cass and the lean man departed as soon as Demetrios stood safe and harmless on the wrong side of Cell 2's metal door. Putney lingered. "I'll tend to your comfort. No talking, mind." He opened a door down the corridor on a storage shed.

"He says no talking," said the bearlike man cross-legged on a heap of straw. "It's kind of like his cough. I'm Bosco."

"Demetrios. How do?"

"Fair to shitty. Glad to know y'."

"No talking!" Putney bustled back with straw on a pitchfork.

"He has this problem," said Bosco. "How to unlock the door without putting down the straw. Give it up, Putney?"

"Up yours too." Putney set down the load and worked the key. "Stand back. This here's a self-service reform school, Mister Fancy—you make your own bed." He flung the straw to the free side of the cell, and leaned on the fork, dim and droopy in the watery light from one barred window high in the north wall. "That all the money you had?"

"Ayah. When do I get to see Lieutenant Brome?"

"Can't figure the way you people come snorting and piss-assing in here without no money. You a'n't that stupid, you'd ought to know it costs like anyplace else. Don't worry about Brome." Putney backed off fretfully, his key rattled in the wards, and he spoke from behind the gate's protection. "Cass or Jack'll get word to your people afterwhile, likely. We're good about that." He giggled. "We a'ways notify the next of skin." A fine, no doubt, and Mam Estelle would feel obliged to pay it. *Trouble walks with me.* "No talking now," said Putney, and he trotted off to his own burrow.

"The gentlemen either side of us are resting," said Bosco. "One beat up and could be dead for all I know; t'other's getting on for a hundred and not too lively— you might hear him sing, or ask for vitamins, whatever

87

they be. Care for a marawan candy? Can't light up nothing in here, account of the straw."

"Thanks, Bosco." Demetrios chewed the aromatic trifle; a light sedative would be welcome. "Been here a while?"

"Long enough to get three days older." Settled on the not uncomfortable straw, Demetrios considered his companion—smooth-flowing muscle, upper arms like a bear's hams. Bosco was hairy but neat, the brown shag of his head somewhat combed. He smelled sweaty but not rancid; probably liked to wash when he got the chance. "Misunderstanding and hard luck brung me low, Demetrios. See, there was this sucking pig come up to the fence when I happened to be leaning over, and I could see he was the one too many in the litter, having a hard time. So I picks him up, and I was going happy down the road planning a short life and a merry one for the dear little fella, when these two cops come out of the bushes, rot them. Same two bastards that brung you in, and don't it beat all Christ the way they hunt in pairs?—Cass alone I could've handled, no trouble. I got my little friend tucked out of sight, but he tickled me working his feet around, the way I couldn't help laughing like somebody'd left me money. This Cass he says, 'I declare to God I think you got a shoat under your coat.' Why, I told the son of a bitch, I says, 'I'm just taking him to his mother, a'n't that all right?' They never believe you if you're from out of town. Then in the follering argument the thin one—that's Jack Jellicoe, meaner'n a cat turd, you want to keep away from him—he leaned his club on the back of my head. I still got the lump, been here three days waiting for the Public Defender to come back from wherever he's resting his arse amongst the lilies, and they got the pig. See, I'd come to think of him as *my* little pig. Bugger me blind if I think the original owner ever saw hide or trotters of him again, and they call this a King's Republic?"

"They do for a fact. From out of town, you said?"

"Born and raised amongst the Ramblers. I might be one of Boss Gammo's own get—of course he said that about every promising sprout in the gang, said it'd been sired by the blunt end of a hurricane and the hurricane was him. Ever hear of Boss Gammo?"

"Why, a caravan gang that called themselves Ramblers came here to Nuber eight years ago. That name rings a bell."

"Do say!" Bosco's heavy face grew alert; sad, too. "Boss Gammo he never cut his hair, tied it behind him with a hempen string. Said it was his strength, like this Simpson or Sampson or somebody."

"That's the man. They only put on one show. Good entertainment I thought—I'm a storyteller by trade myself —but then some crud started a riot, heads got cracked, the police ran them out of town. Since then all Ramblers have been turned away from the Nuber border posts."

"If that a'n't just like a King's Republic! Eight years ago? Four years after I left 'em. Was his hair a-whitening? Gammo?"

"Pepper-and-salt. But I got only a glimpse of him, Bosco."

"Aye-so." The big man rocked himself back and forth on the straw, assailed by grief. "Eight and four is twelve, a'n't it? And I must be crowding thirty, like. Why, I could lick Boss Gammo now, if I'd ever catch up with the lot. See, Demetrios, I figured to lick him when I was eighteen, but that was too soon, and when the stars quit twinkling inside my brains so's I could get up off the ground, Boss Gammo he says to me, 'Bosco, there a'n't no room for you and me both. You'd come up ahint me one day,' he says. I won't say I wouldn't't've. Picked on me, that man did, oncet he prac'ly grabbed off a girl right out from under me. 'Come back,' he says, 'when you think you're big enough and damfool enough, we'll talk about it some more.' Why, I could lick him now for sure, only I can't find 'em. Last year I chased a rumor up into Adirondack Island. I been here and there—Jasus, I've even lived honest now and then. With a lumber gang, and up to the iron mines at Halloway, oarsman a while onto the Albany ferry—that's nearabout slavery, that is."

"I hear there are several Rambler gangs nowadays."

"But Gammo's is the one and only original. Boss Gammo he thunk up the whole idear—mule-wagons, singers, tumblers, news-carrying, fortune-telling, the whole bit. Them others don't amount to shit alongside Gammo's. I

could've joined one if I wanted. It's like laid onto me, I
got to catch up with Gammo's. Sometimes I get thinking,
what if Gammo he's gone and died on me, the way I'll
never have no other chance to beat up on the old son of
a whore. They wouldn't change the name, bound to be
still Gammo's Ramblers. What if it was Bosco's, hey?
Bosco's Ramblers, how's that sound?"

"Sounds great."

Through the waning of the afternoon Bosco talked on
about a world that Demetrios knew of as though it hung
like a distorting curtain between him and the vanished
other truths of Old Time. There are pirates in the little
islands of Moha Water who take an almost fixed per-
centage of the trade between Adirondack Island and the
republic of Moha that precariously owns it. *Angus, could
you not come to me?*

Except when they steal children or women, or torture
a captain for information about other shipping, that's
almost a comfortable sort of piracy there in Moha Water,
like a goddamn tax, nothing like the vicious operations in
the southern Hudson Sea. Down there the buccaneers have
virtually closed the area to all vessels except the most swift
and well-armed, and so now the pirates range in search
of victims far up and down the coast, and some time soon
the King's Republic will have to clean them out, which
means a navy and likely a small war. Some say the people
of Conicut are hand in glove with 'em. *Solitaire . . .
Paisan . . .* Yet the world that Bosco was idly holding up
for him to see had its own power, its own pull.

Red bear are seen more and more often these days on
Adirondack Island. Bosco himself had been shown the
pelt of one at a settlement called Saubel, and it covered
the whole floor of a twelve by fifteen room, no lie . . . In
Vairmount they are plagued by a kind of wolf like nothing
anyone heard of before, monstrous, black, long in the leg
and (folk say) supernaturally clever as the Devil himself . . . Bosco had heard—but was not sure he believed
the tale—of an isolated family somewhere in Hampsher
completely destroyed by a swarm of the small red-brown
rats, that acted like a swarm of ants . . . In Main, or any-

how somewhere in eastern New England, there's a tribe that worships the brown tiger, calling him Eye of Fire . . .

Slowly in gray-green light the afternoon perished, dwindled from the barred window. Putney brought a dinner of stew and flabby tea. In Cell 3, soft snoring shifted to tremulous ancient song:

> "I hope to read my title clear
> To mansions in the skies—"

—and again, without change, and again. When Putney set food in there, the old voice pleaded: "I want my vitamins. I want my vitamins. I want my vitamins."

On the far side of the corridor, well beyond any reach from the cells, Putney placed two tallow candles that might sputter half the night. "I want my vitamins. . . ." No sound came from Cell 1. Putney hastily slapped down a plate in there and backed out muttering something Demetrios could not interpret.

"Some day, Put," said Bosco, "you better give Gran'dad his vitamins. What be they anyhow?"

"None of your mothering business," said Putney in an evil temper, and slammed the door again between his privacy and theirs.

An hour faded, and the barred window high in the wall was giving on a darkness profound and starless, yet there must have been a field of brilliance beyond the shroud of the oaks. Demetrios and Bosco had shoved their dirty plates under the door, where Putney collected them in glum silence; the old man in Cell 3 was snoring, the other cell as dead in quiet as before; Putney's door slammed again and no more was heard from him. A breeze drifted through the window, cooling the cell, touching the candles in the corridor with a restlessness. Their warm small light, abandoning Bosco to the shadows, shone on the verticals of the bars with illusion of softness. You could push your hand clear through them. Someone had.

Two hands, rather small. The fingers curled over the metal, pale separate lights. A face was pressing close to the barricade deeply shadowed by it, and it was rounded like

91

Garth's with heavy eyebrows under yellow hair, but more delicate, with a certain sweet recklessness that Garth had left behind him or perhaps never allowed himself. "Ssst! Hey! Demetrios!"

By standing on tiptoe Demetrios could bring his eyes level with the boy's. "You must be Frankie." The eyes sparkled with the delights of danger.

"Garth's here too. I'm like sitting on his neck."

"I can't hardly gosemplace anywhere without the Plague coming along," said Garth, unseen. "Be you by lone, Demetrios?"

"You'd be lost without me, Clunk. You know I'm the brains of the outfit. No, there's another ga with him."

"You can trust me, kid," said Bosco, moving on silent bear-feet to the door of the cell where he could watch the corridor. "I'll keep looksy, Demetrios—go ahead and talk to your friends."

Frankie frowned a question about him; Demetrios nodded—Bosco wouldn't peach on a fellow jailbird. Demetrios strained higher, trying to see Garth; the sill was too wide. Close at his ear Frankie murmured: "Going to spring you, duck-soupy it is."

"Lordy! I'd have to get out of town then."

"We all go," whispered Frankie. "You, me, the Clunk —me and the Clunk got nothing but hell at home since Ma died, the way he keeps bringing home them dirty pigs and never sober—"

"Come on, Plague, he don't want to hear about that. But that's how it is, Demetrios, we all want out. Mister Angus he's shook up—"

"You've seen him?"

"Sure have. Listen, there's a purge going in Inner City. His mother—oh, he'll tell you about it. They're after him too. He slipped out the north gate last night, him and the dog, had to knock out a guard. By daylight he worked around through the woods to the Redcurtain Street side, took a chance asking his way to Mam Estelle's, you was gone when he got there. Mam Estelle hid him up safe. I talked to him there after I seen what happened at the Meadows. Mister Angus come, see, for to tell you it's worse for you than you thought. Heard people talking about you. Calling you an Abramite and a foreign spy. It's the Abramites they're purging, only that ain't all."

*Then Angus—Angus—*"A spy from Missouri no doubt."

"Huh? Oh—yeah. This purge is the big one, he said to tell you. We better all get out, nothing else to do."

"What was it about his mother?"

"She—I druther he told you, Demetrios. She's like, with them people doing the purge. They're—*killing* the Abramites, in Inner City. And some others they don't like. Well, Mister Angus didn't want to risk drawing trouble on Mam Estelle, so he'll be out in the woods now, him and the dog, and the Professor, and your woman. Me and Frankie come here to get the layout of this place. Only that one old fart minding it tonight?"

"Only him," said Bosco, turning his head. "Couldn't help listening. It's dead as a tomb here all night long. Count on me, boys—I'll lend a hand. Nobody wants out more'n I do."

"Me and Angus will be back."

"And me," said Frankie.

"Okay," said Demetrios to all of them, feeling frightened and old, and shaken by the miracle of love redeemed. "Okay."

"After we spring you," said Garth, "we join your woman and the Professor and Frankie at a place I know on the South Road."

"No, I come back with you and Mister Angus to spring him," said Frankie. His hands jumped from the bars. "Hey! Clumsy!"

"We'll see. Le' go my hair, Plague."

"Balls to we'll see. You got to have the brains of the outfit with you. Besides, this is the happenest day of my life."

"We'll *see*," said Garth, and Frankie's face receded in darkness, a candle going out.

Bosco said: "You really got friends." He spoke with envy.

"You'll come with us? We could do with another friend."

"I'm your man. Where will you go, you think?"

93

"West—ah, I don't know. We must all decide. I dream of going west—and yet it'll all be under water, the places I knew."

"Like Gammo's Ramblers—into my head all the time and won't let go. You be an Old-Timer?"

"Thirteen when the bombs fell. Loved one world, feel lost in the other. But the old one's gone. Downstream with time."

*My Mam Estelle wrote no more in her diary that day, though she was not with the great corn spirit, indeed she didn't work in much afternoon tea of any kind. By seven the place was jumping with evening customers and the girls working their ass off to coin a phrase, and right up to then Mam Estelle had been Busy, too busy and worried to write the Story of her Life, and so am I, so am I who write this book, for I must tell how Angus the son of Steven came to the side door of Mam Estelle's Public Entertainment Facility like any tradesman or beggar, and was admitted by the girl named Solitaire, who saw how grief and anger were clawing his heart and chewing his vitals, and weariness riding him like the black ape, and his own great gray hound could not protect him. It busies me and worries me—the passions always do—I ought to be carving cherrystones with the Lord's Prayer, but God, there's no living in it.*

*"Will he come in then?" says Solitaire, and he did, into the kitchen where Mam Estelle was sitting with some innocent morning tea—no corn spirit neither, just her last peaceful cup of the day—came in with a backward look for the alley like a man pursued, and he asked for Demetrios, and was told man Demetrios had gone to the Town Hall hours since and was not returned. "That's bad," said Angus.*

*Solitaire was looking into him, she in her slavey's smock, gray smudge on her cheek, turban of grubby cloth about her hair, and she said: "He is scratched with brambles. One time Solitaire was scratched with brambles and she saw a hole in the brook that had no bottom, the water ran black out of the heart of the earth—will he come sit down and rest, himself it is?" And Angus saw through his*

94

own pain that she was concerned for him in a way that (he thought) no one before had ever been concerned.

She touched Brand's head. The dog whined gently and leaned his shoulder against her little thigh, too polite to fling up his paws on her slenderness. "He likes you," said Angus. "Don't be afraid of him or me." The slavey's disguise was a nothing to be sure, a curtain for other people. He looked through it, scarce aware of it, discovering the heart of strangeness.

She said: "Solitaire is not afraid. Oh, she found loving-kindness here a while ago. But what happened to hurt him?"

She could astonish him. Through shock and exhaustion after the night of violence—after all we know, and you might as well also, that his mother had bedded Senator Pry, the coming man of the hour and King Brian's instrument in the purge, which was somewhat like pissing on his father's memory, and for Angus the graciousness of life in Inner City had been ripped away like the cover from a sewer—through his misery Angus understood that Solitaire was asking about himself. "Oh," he said, "I saw the black waters too. I knew they were there, I must have known it."

"Well," said Mam Estelle, "sit down, sit down. Pull up a chair for some tea, and what do you want with our man Demetrios?"

"I must warn him." Soon they had the necessary information out of him—his name, his place in the crazy world, his meeting with Demetrios—or I should say that Mam Estelle did, for Solitaire asked no questions, only moved about watching him, now from the light, now from the sun-shadow. You might have thought her transparent, a ghost of smudged beauty blown here and there, a captive light driven by the turning of a mirror.

She saw a boy with red-brown hair, who wore no white tunic now though surely born to it but a gray jacket like a workman's, a gray loincloth, luxurious sandals. On his wrist was a fantastic little watch, clearly of Old Time, at his belt a leather-sheathed knife; at his back he carried no bow nor quiver, but one of those long carry-alls—where

*I come from we call them bac-pacs. She saw a face of
beauty and gravity—boy, man, angel, no need to wonder
—coming to her out of nowhere, in trouble and in need
of her.*

*He saw a girl wearing innocent secrets like protective
garments; so he would always think of her, even when
secrets were put aside.*

*Forgive me if I rush you along so. I do promise to fill
you in on all the Facts that you so clearly have a right to
know in all their bustling factiness. But to me your novelist
the essential thing is what Mam Estelle saw: that Solitaire
was no wraith at all but a woman in love. It can happen
to anyone—pity we are so seldom warned. And Mam
Estelle saw it had happened to Angus at the same time—
one of the rarest coincidences in this world, in most of the
worlds I know.*

"What part of the west you from, Demetrios?"

"Missouri. They called it midwest in those days. Have
you traveled much in that direction?"

"Not much. Couple years ago I got as far as the coast
of the Freshwater Sea—that's what the trappers call it; I
was with a party of them, for the season. Our base camp
was near a puny little settlement called Shatawka, mainly
goddamn natives. They called the sea Lake Erie and said
you could drink it. I tried it—try anything once—Jasus!
Never trust a native. Inland though, the brooks and springs
are pretty fair. It's bad earthquake country. No heavy
shocks but small ones day after day like God or somebody
couldn't quit growling to himself. They say one day he'll
throw a big one. The beaver don't mind—real thick around
there and north of there. We got silver fox too, and marten
—of course the damned red rats rob your traps all-a-time.
Game's easy to get. There was a brown tiger scare while
we was there—robbed a village to the north, but we never
saw him. I never have seen him, wonder sometimes if he's
folk-say . . ."

A casual, throaty voice, an innocent-seeming, blunt,
thirtyish face in the candlelight—Demetrios warmed to
him. Himself unsure and tense, as if already gone forth to
dare the roads and the wilderness with diminishing strength

96

and no sight of a goal, he found Bosco's talk sustaining. Bosco was no storyteller: he knew these things directly with his senses and with very little imagination—the feel of an enslaved hand on the oar; the gloom, acrid stench, and peril of a mine; the stillness of jungle that is no stillness but a teeming of life, the passion latent in the overabundance, a patience like a serpent's hot slow patience, a waiting that may break forth in a roaring or a cry, but only for a reason. It made the hour pass—

> "I hope to read my title clear
> To mansions in the skies—"

"Does he ever sing anything else?"

"Not since I been here, just them two lines. That and his vitamins. He's got like a home here, Putney says—ever' time they turn him loose he quick does something dirty so to get himself back in. You know—nourishing stew, no worries except about his vitamins, whatever they be. Cell 1—that's different. They brung that man in late last night, flung him there—he couldn't hardly walk. Not a sound out of him except breathing for a while. I hollered to him and pounded on the wall, no good, nor I couldn't get anything out of Putney, just gibbering. Ha'n't even heard the breathing since about the time they brung you in. That dish Put took away hadn't been touched. They let people die accidental-apurpose, here at Nuber?"

"I never thought so." *What do you know about anything, Demetrios, you who filled your mind with fancies and farewells while another world grew up around you—*

"Maybe it's just Put. Real burrow-cat, that man. The ga in there could be dead for days while Put waits for the brass to tell him what to do. Hark!—"

A muffled disturbance in Putney's room—in a moment the door opened, releasing stronger candlelight and a glimpse of Putney himself, popeyed on his cot, bound and gagged. A dog, a boy, and a man hurried to the cell door, while Garth remained on guard over Putney. Angus shoved his stocking mask in his gray jacket. Stiff-legged beside him with lifted hackles, Brand studied the dark, sorted

97

the smells. "Damn this thing!" Angus was struggling with the key.

"That'n' maybe," said Frankie correctly. Angus flung open the door. "Brains of the outfit," said the boy in the mask.

Angus caught Demetrios in a quick embrace, kissing both unshaven cheeks. "I was afraid for you. Have they—"

"No, nothing bad, I'm all right." Dizziness swirled in him. Who ever knows joy or pain in the moment of their presence? Only the differing intensities of light; later, remembering, we give them names. "This is Bosco, who wants to come with us. He knows wilderness, and the roads, places we never heard of."

"Step closer, Bosco, will you? I'm nearsighted." Bosco moved into the field of ruthless inspection. Angus the polite, confused boy of yesterday was surely not gone, but merely hidden in Angus the commander because there was no time for him. "All right—good. Come with us." There seemed no question of challenging Angus's right to decide. In this crisis someone must be ready with swift rational aye or no: let it be Angus, who said that power stinks, but who understood the exercise of it.

"I'm in for ripping off a sucking pig, Mister."

"Maybe I'll ask you to teach me how it's done. Got any left?"

"Cops got it." Bosco was looking into Cell 1, and as Demetrios was about to join him there he muttered from his mouth-corner: "Keep the kid out of here."

The man in Cell 1 sprawled naked on the floor, mouth open, his clotted wounds untended; his chest was motionless, and Demetrios knew him. Demetrios turned away and slipped his arm over Frankie's shoulders. "We'll go talk to Garth." Passing Angus, he indicated Cell 1 with a motion of his eyes. "Holman Shawn."

In Putney's room Garth stood watch by the outer door, the eyeholes of his mask a blue sparkle. "Okay, man Demetrios?"

"Okay, Garth."

"About your dream, my aunt said—" Garth glanced at Putney's flushed listening face. "Well, later."

"I want my vitamins. I want my vitamins."

98

"You'll get your vitamins, o' man," said Bosco's genial voice.

"Will I then? God bless you.

> "I hope to read my title clear
> To mansions in the skies—"

From the curve of Demetrios's arm Frankie looked up, demanding answers. "What was it in t'other cell you didn't want me to see?"

Demetrios could remember: at twelve only a fool doesn't know that the other side of the coin is sorrow; and Frankie would never be a fool. "A dead man, Frankie. He was an Abramite. They left him there after a beating; they let it happen." Frankie stared, eyes bottomless; the ocean is not concerned with forgiveness. "It's the other side, Frankie. The other side of the happenest day of our lives."

# CHAPTER NINE

## I only come to see You on your Way

> *They say an artist must represent his times. They
> don't say why; maybe they think the mirror creates
> the image. If the artist objects, Procrustes is always
> ready with his rusty, trusty, snaggletooth hacksaw.*
> —*DEMETRIOS.*

A mist often rises from the ground in the nights at
Nuber, flowing about the houses, which stand lonely—
houses always do: islands that people have shoveled together for resting-places of the journey. The mist absorbs
the earth-loving touch of footsteps, the sound of laughter
under the breath, whispered love and courage. The mist is
ambiguity and marvel. One breathes it in as vapor and
becomes—let us say, wiser: at least a blurred wisdom is
to be found in the fog, an ability to say what might never
be said in daylight or under the extravagant invitations of
the moon.

Along alleys and avenues where even the trees were
drowsing, the ground mist joined a vapor that rolled in
through an eastern gap in the hills. Night smelled of salt
air, of wild ocean loneliness. Fog yielded sometimes to
persuasion of a late candle in a window, or thinned to
reveal the thrust of a building's corner, a hitching post, a
front-yard fence. In all this passage Garth and Frankie
were the guides. To Demetrios they conveyed an intima-
tion of the medieval; their ash bows and quivers were part
of them, practical as any 20th Century soldier's rifle. Both
knew every turning as a fox knows his own hillside, knew
every step from the sad shack where they had been born,
in the shadow of King Brian's Wall, to the Great South

100

Road. That section where the Meadows end, allowing the city to heave up against the Wall, is called Outer Wall Street; some of the shacks lean three-sided against the mass itself, and rain trickles through the haphazard joining. The boys' father, when he worked, was a street-scavenger, selling the manure to farmers at starveling prices.

Demetrios walked behind, now and then touching their shirts or hip satchels for comfort. The walnut stick satisfied his right hand. Behind him came Angus, Brand, and Bosco.

"Have we far to go tonight?" Having spoken, Demetrios was disgusted by that elderly querulous noise from his throat. Angus could not have slept at all during the past night, when the purge began; he would have been traversing the rim of hell while Demetrios lay with Solitaire and the Professor snug in bed.

"Not far, Demetrios." Angus spoke gently. "We thought when we've joined the others we'll go on to the hant-house off the South Road and rest there, till first-light anyway. I hear nobody goes near it for fear of getting bespooked."

"Good enough."

"We mustn't stay there long, Mister Angus," said Garth. "They could set hounds on Demetrios's trail, or yours, the way dogs won't usu'ly stop for spooks, nor men won't by daylight maybe."

"There are even some in Inner City who don't believe in 'em." The undercurrent in Angus' voice was not all amusement. "Like me."

"Aye-so?" Garth's voice was troubled, the trouble echoed by an uncertain throat-noise from Bosco back there in the dark—not so deep a dark: a moon was exerting power above the mist, so that the travelers might feel like swimmers rising to the surface into new dimensions of breath and motion. "Man Demetrios, my aunt asked the book about your dream. It said the railroad was a dream-speech —see, that's the science of the—the subconscience, and the real road is going to go over water for sure on a long journey. The book did say that, each time she let it fall open, and she read it right out to me—that is, I don't mean *read,* but anyhow she knowed that was what it like meant."

101

"My thanks to her," said Demetrios, remembering the age of science. For more than a century it had been able to hold in check, somewhat, the human compulsion to accept the dithering of primitive magic as revelation and mystic truth. It could not teach its method of approach except to the very few—(how hard did it try?—Demetrios wasn't sure); nor could it suppress the corruption generated by the gifts that science itself had tossed to fools possessed of power—how hard did it try? By the time computers were being employed in the commercial development of astrology, tarot, witchcraft, all the rest of the dreary sludge— by that time, long before 1993, maybe we were already done for. "We shall cross water," said Demetrios, "and grow older." He hoped that Garth's love-sensitive ear would not catch the sarcasm and anger that had threatened to erupt through his words like a belch from an acid stomach.

*Garth is kind, lovable, good. Didn't he just help me get out of a stinking jail? When was I appointed to turn him into a 20th Century rationalist, in an age that hates reason, supposing I knew how it could be done? All the same—*

*What is there to hope for? What can we do? Accept the new dark age as inevitable in the rhythm of history?*

*Periods of special enlightenment do tend to be short— Greece, the European Renaissance—and then the poor startled human race must go pottering back into the cave to digest. False analogies: the human race is not a person, and forgetfulness is hardly digestion.*

*So—we hope, we make believe that reason can somehow nourish light in private places, through more long dismal centuries when nothing is certain except the power of unreason? What else?*

The moonlight explaining the face of Frankie grew tender.

*Why, damn it, Garth is teachable, as teachable as Frankie, or Angus. What if I AM appointed? Self-appointed—it's for me to say. Sort out your own brains first, Demetrios: beginning now.*

"This'll be the South Road," said Garth. The mist, no higher than their knees, ran as a river of silent whiteness channeled between walls of maple and evergreen and oak,

102

and the blue-black summits of leaves were sprinkled and sparkling with stars.

*Men wanted those; dreamed of approaching them. They did reach the moon; they did send astounding gadgets to the wastes of Venus, Mars, Jupiter to listen and scan and crackle reports back to the home planet where they were playing with tarot cards and nerve gas and leaky nuclear toys.*

*Axiom in man-made ethics: Human beings choose their own purposes, according to whatever complex of desire and information dominates their thinking. Corollary: The purposes will be good (by whatever standard of "good" is being employed) insofar as the desire is good and the information sound. Conclusion (one of many): An old man possessed of relatively trustworthy information cannot be lightly excused from the obligation to teach. . . . Define "trustworthy." Define "obligation" . . . oh, I am bumbling. I am getting old. . . .*

The ventriloquial laughterlike noise of a screech owl trilled out of milky obscurity ahead of them at the side of the road, two calls close together. The sound was immediately answered—from all around him, it seemed to Demetrios, but he saw Frankie's lips in slight motion, and then the strengthening half-moon displayed the bounty of Frankie's grin. Demetrios whispered: "Solitaire did that?"

"Learnt her this afternoon," said Frankie. "Brains of the outfit." He called softly: "Everything's okay. It's us."

A three-bodied shadow emerged, into the mist that seemed about to dissolve yet never did, quite, as though something of it—a softness, a blurring of vision like the myopia of Angus Bridgeman or the hesitations of Demetrios, would always accompany the travelers, quieting the human lust for certainties—and became three separate souls, carrying small packs, daring night and wilderness, young and not young. Here was small sweet Solitaire, and the Professor carrying his lute close-wrapped against the dampness; a thicker, heavier shape turned to the moon the watchful face of Babette.

Angus spoke under his breath. "You know these friends, Brand." Brand lowered his ears, trotting forward smoke-

103

silent. Solitaire reached, to speak to him with her hand. The company was eight.

"O Demetrios!" Solitaire did not kiss him. She pressed her face on his chest and held him fast, making his lank body a refuge. "Demetrios, Demetrios, sacred to the Earth."

"My name—you knew that, love?"

"Demetrios forgets what he's told her. Solitaire never forgets anything—except herself." Frankie and Garth watched the road in both directions—no one ever travels the roads at night, even the Great South Road: almost no one; no one respectable. "Solitaire has a thing to tell—not now— soon—sometime. Demetrios will make a happiness out of it, could be. Solitaire wants to carry a stick like Demetrios. The Professor is thinking somebody will cut a stick for Solitaire to carry."

"Somebody better," said Babette. "Man Demetrios, bless you, I only come to see you on your way, then I got to go back to my Mam, the way she wouldn't last three days without me."

The company was, in a way, seven. But more than that still, for one of the amazing aspects of love is the traffic it carries on with memory—*now I know this for true, I who write this book, for once upon a time an ancient man, I being then not much bigger than a fly-speck, took me on his lap and said: "Here's a howdy-do! What's a howdy-do? A howdy-do's a little one, a howdy-do's a pretty one, and here's a howdy-do!" I reached and got me a fistful of white beard with a kiss in it. Now the love of my father and mother and some others had surrounded me the way the sea moves in perfection around a little fish, but in that moment with Whitebeard (I haven't a notion who he was, never did know) I discovered how the universe holds separate beings who can open their own countries of love to let you in a while. So Whitebeard goes with me; but those I couldn't like—why, I treat 'em hatefully: I forget 'em.* Demetrios would carry Babette in himself the whole way, whatever that way was (even now wondering, Shall I ever see her again after tonight?)—her broad bosom, her cheerful directness, round face, open smile.

Angus asked: "May I borrow the hatchet?"

"For sure," said Garth, watching the road. "Any time, Mister Angus, yourself it is. Frankie——?"

Frankie unslung from his belt the small camp-ax of Old Time. He removed the leather guard, and the blade's edge became under the moon an arc of fierce frost. It was evident, in the language of Frankie's hands, that to him the care of the Hatchet was a most holy trust; also that he did not understand why Mister Angus and not himself or Garth should make use of it.

"Man Garth," said Angus, "let it be Mister Angus no more. I have no place in the Inner City nor want none, nor any place I know of at all except in this company."

Garth watched the road. "Aye-so, Angus. Try the oak yonder, where it leans out a branch." Frankie set the Hatchet in Angus's hand, and went with him, pulling down the branch for Angus to cut, staying close at his side while Angus trimmed it with a natural bend for a handle, and then returned the Hatchet.

Then Frankie must rub the edge of it with his shirt. "That Hatchet," said Angus, "has had good care." Frankie nodded, speechless, finding it no occasion for a grin, only for a different sort of smile that glowed and vanished in the white light. Angus brought the stick to Solitaire. She moved out of Demetrios's arms to take it and weigh it in her hand. "It's green," said Angus. "It will ripen."

"Everything does," she said. "The stones, and the stars. Now Solitaire can lean on a staff if she's tired or lazy or cross."

"We must get on," said Garth. "Frankie, watch with me for the wood-road to the hant-house. I might miss it."

"The white stone, remember?" But when the Company had moved on a few hundred slow paces along the open misty channel of the South Road, it was Frankie who said: "There it be. Leave me take front, the way I see best in the dark. You link up one and one behind."

"It's more'n an hour you ha'n't called me Clunk."

Many moments later (not a measurable time) as the Company moved ahead through what was for Demetrios a tunnel of unbroken darkness, his finger hooked in Garth's belt, Solitaire's in his, the other links a chain of nerves

105

that made them (for a while) one body, Frankie's small treble reached Demetrios: "It'll be never again you call me Plague." Then sometimes Frankie's voice was warning, clear enough so that Bosco at the end of the line would hear it: "Stick in the path crossways." Or: "Briers, briers." Or: "Fallen log, don't nobody tumble." Then at last (clearly not a measurable time): "Brains of the outfit sees moonlight ahead—" at which a fleet ripple of laughter ran through the Company, since Frankie himself had sent the remark down the line with a chuckle in it.

Entering the pallid clearing behind Garth and Frankie, Demetrios did not immediately see the hant-house, for it crouched at the darkest edge of the moonlit space where the forest had flung around it wanton arms of wild grape, and pushed through its front courtyard the shaft of a pine now twice the height of the building, but could not quite capture the ancient thing—not altogether, not yet. His eyes discovered a splash of moonlight on a surface of slate that nature had never arranged, and three eyes of glassless windows above the mute scream of a doorless doorway. Garth said reflectively: "It's them stone floors inside. Been no place for seeds to find a crack, or they'd 'a' done it like that pine wherever a mite of sun come through."

"Colonial?" said Demetrios. "By God I think so. I never knew it was here. I could have dreamed a story for it."

"No reason to know," said Garth. "We're more'n a mile from the South Road now and nobody comes here. What's Colonial?"

"Old Old-Time, before the—call it the age of marvels. This house may have been erected more than three hundred years ago."

"There's a Colonial house in the Inner City," said Angus. "It's been kept in repair. They call it the Dutch Museum."

"Dutch," said Bosco. "That was another name for them bloody Injans. Nay, I seen an old house at Albany, I think they called it Colonial, only the gov'ment don't let you go into it."

Solitaire shivered in the crook of Demetrios's arm; Babette had made the sign of the Wheel. "Ah, they were all just people," said Demetrios, "and long gone; and this

106

is just a building that didn't fall apart easily." A barn owl blurted his call and came floating out of an upper window to carry a shadow across the moon. "How good are the walls, Garth?"

"Good—stone. With what's left of a wood and plaster finish onto the inside, only people must've took to stealing bits and pieces till there a'n't much left. Roof slates too, they be near-about gone at the back—nay, Frankie, don't!" —for Frankie had swaggered near the black doorway and was talking like an owl: "You who hoo-hoo! Anybody to ho-huh-home?" At Garth's protest he demanded: "A'n't we going in?"

The hant-house stood calm in its three hundred years. They heard aeolian murmurs, a rustling of whatever modest life had chosen in this century to make a home here. The Professor joined Frankie protectively by the doorway. Bosco was grumbling: "We got anything for lights? I wouldn't mind the place with a bit of light."

"Got some pine torches and carrier in my pack," said Garth.

"Solitaire could light one," said Solitaire.

"All right." All of them including himself, Demetrios realized, had been waiting on that approval from Angus. In the shelter of Angus's spread jacket Solitaire won a flame from her tinderbox. Two golden faces confronted one another on their own island of light. So deeply tranced was Solitaire in her discoveries that Garth must touch her hand, reminding her of the torch he held waiting.

These are good inventions in their way, pine sticks with a tight binding of rag sometimes impregnated with pine oil —turpentine if you insist. The stick is whittled so it may be inserted in a slotted device like a candlestick, which can be stuck in the ground or in a wall-bracket; around the slot is a guard like the hilt of a rapier, intended to protect the carrying hand. A good torch will burn prettily and rather calmly for quite a while. The age of electricity could easily have mass-produced these foodiddles for sale as antiques, but history says that to its everlasting loss it didn't—something about fire underwriters.

Garth held up his good torch. The Company followed him into the quiet place.

## CHAPTER TEN

*—if I can teach you to be patient—*

> *Those very ones who believe that everything has been
> said and done, will greet you as new and yet will close
> the door behind you. And then they will say again
> that everything has been said and done.*
> *—Eugène Delacroix, JOURNAL, 1824.*

Garth's pine torch, its bracket wedged into a firedog of
the hearth, shone on the face of Angus, who sat with
Brand stretched out beside him. Demetrios watched that
dear image with drowsing eyes. What of the poison of
jealousy, the making of demands, the sin of possessiveness?
Surely an old man might keep his heart clear of those
follies, at least among these gentle few. Must grief inevitably burn because there is one who loves and one who
is loved? One compensates. For Angus and Solitaire it
was a little different: for a time they would be caught
in the same fever. He remembered how something like
this had once glowed for him and Elizabeth of Hartford,
and might still hold warmth if she had not died. Death
had blown it away, and now he found he could not quite
recall the color of her eyes.

The Professor's lute sent questions into cobwebbed
corners, driving out echoes to play hide-and-seek. The small
torch opened the ceiling of the big room to infinity.
Solitaire sat by Demetrios on their blanket, and Babette
was cross-legged on his other side, her plump shadow
dancing on the wall with the shadows of Angus and
Solitaire; Demetrios could see her broad kind face if he
turned his head. He was going to miss her, if they went
west through the wilderness. He would miss Mam Estelle,

the girls, even Nuber itself, having consigned forty-seven years of his life to the peculiar place.

Bosco, ready to grab comfort anywhere, had rolled up in Garth's blanket while Garth and Frankie took first watch. After it Angus and Bosco would watch until first-light, and then, Angus had suggested, they might as well follow a wood-road that wound southwest from the hant-house, paralleling the Great South Road in its beginning. The South Road itself would be unsafe for fugitives, up to the border of Katskil. Garth and Frankie had once tried that wood-road for a mile, running away from home. Their mother was still living then: love and conscience drove them back.

Before the last flower of the torch had fallen Demetrios entered sleep. Westward chugged the homely locomotive, the woodburner with bulging stack, westward past Aberedo, clattering, coughing dirt. It halted at a water tower, where a man with *Abel Kane* embroidered on his overalls warned the engine-driver: "Careful, man, the water short-age is terrible. Thing is They got to cover the earth with with, and that don't leave much. Can't turn back the clock to Noah, no sir. Likely won't nobody know where he's at till They've done the—uh—hydraulic finalizing."

*(I your novelist know quite well where I'm at. My prob-lem is to know where I'm atn't.)*

The woman with the market basket leaned across Demetrios to ask a deaf farmer: "What'd the man say?" A sad little girl with adenoids and a goiter in the seat opposite watched with never a smile. Demetrios replied for the deaf man, or wanted to: "We're going to Hester-ville to see the Water Shortage." She wasn't listening. The sad child's mother stared through Demetrios with dislike. But here already was Hesterville—All out for Hestervi-i-ille!

No way out except down into flat green water, down and down, since the station loomed there below. The train puffed along an embankment, the passengers floated out and down like Demetrios, off the open carriage with the wicker seats—open air, smoky air, lost air—into green water deep and slow. White shapes stood tranquil in green water-air; darker shapes roved up with unknown intent—

109

we all live in darkness, don't we?—*and in gross darkness the people*—

"Demetrios." Solitaire spoke gently. "Demetrios made noises." She rubbed his forehead softly, a service she had done before when nightmare trod on him. Confusion drained away. The silly dream was a face gone in a crowd. Ambiguous light was entering the hant-house, whether from dawn or a descending moon he could not tell. The face of Angus he could not find. Where it had been a scar in the wall appeared: plaster had fallen from lath in a patch the shape of North America, and in front of this hung a spider, a good gray scavenging citizen nursing her drop of poison and her own torch of life. Frankie was lying with his head in Solitaire's lap, looking in sleep more like nine years old than twelve. "Angus and Bosco be watching outside."

"Is it moonlight?"

"No, day begins. A bird called. Talk soft so Love can sleep."

"Redbird it were," said Babette, her voice as low as Solitaire's in awe of Frankie's slumber. "I can see my way home soon spite of fog."

"Can't come with us?—nay, I know. The Mam needs you."

"Wouldn't last a day and me not there. Will I tell her you'll come back?—oyah, of course I will, I mean, will there be truth in it?"

"How can I say? Do old men ever come back?"

"Shame on you, Dimmy!" said Babette, and shook him. "Shame on you for a gloomer! Come on, come out of the bad dreams!"

Demetrios sat up, accepting the morning chill. "Yes—yes, we must find a place where they don't require a license for storytelling." Light was showing him the shape of the ancient structure, once maybe a reception room for gentry in wigs and knee breeches. A stairway curve broke into darkness short of the second floor; the upper landing had dropped, likely decayed by years of leakage from the roof. A heap of plaster and rotted wood lay below the break. "We must look for a place where things can be made better without making them worse."

110

Solitaire's fingertips spoke love to Frankie's curls, not waking him. He moved, a vague thrust of hips against the blanket, and quieted, his parted mouth a poem of Eros. "Solitaire has a thing to tell . . . Solitaire is pregnant."

"Oh—"

"By Demetrios," she said, smiling at him in the growing light. "She planned it. She knows her calendar." The lute chuckled from a shadowed place. "For a month she and Professor only played games outside the door. Paisan is saying he planned it with her. So there'd be seed of Demetrios."

Elizabeth of Hartford, her wasted agony, the horror of the birth and double death—yet there was that half-chance, that bloodless statistical encouragement: Elizabeth's own genes might have been the ones to carry the 20th Century damnation. *Most births are still normal—three out of five, isn't that what they say?—when they occur at all—otherwise who would try to prolong the days before extinction?* "Solitaire—my love Solitaire—two months? Three?"

"Nearer three," said Solitaire with pride.

"We'll get out of Katskil, settle in a safe place to wait your time." *Safe place!—where is that?* "Babette, stay away from the Abramites. At Town Hall I was questioned about Abramites at Mam Estelle's. Told 'em nothing of course. Fran ought to get out of town."

"Leave it to me. Don't *worry!*" She added quaint Old-Time words that folk still deprecatingly used: "Do your own thing, Dimmy."

Angus came in with light around him, rousing Garth, kneeling by Frankie and Solitaire, silently asking: *Is it well with us?* It was the bow-boy blind with sleep whose shoulder he kissed, Frankie whose hair he rudely rumpled, Demetrios of whom he asked gently: "Shall we go by the wood-road?"

Solitaire kindled a small fire in the hearth, where Babette toasted bread and bacon. She had brought along other more practical food to start the journey—dried corn and fruit, smoked meat, hard meal-cakes, a flask of wine. Angus had money with him; Garth and Bosco and Frankie claimed skill at hunting and fishing. All the same Babette

111

cried a little, watching them go, in the morning fog that was both confusion and a shelter, down that road which might turn in any direction, maybe toward nowhere. She watched them go—sharp-eyed Garth and Frankie, her old weird Demetrios, sweet mad Solitaire with her branch of oak gaily mimicking the old man's staff—indeed she, with maybe the most to lose, seemed to be the happiest to be going (but how old was Solitaire, really?—Babette had never felt sure)—and dark-browed Angus with the gray hound who was more like a part of himself than a servant, and the massive soft-footed stranger Bosco who—Babette considered him tricky: his watchful face was telling nothing of his inward life. Babette watched them go, gave her nose a last wipe on the back of her arm, disconsolately plodded back to her share of the work of the world.

*(But much later she rejoined us, as I will tell if I can teach you to be patient with me.)*

[Saturday, July 20]

*So they went off into the Fog, Babette says, about sun-up, and from what The Boy told us when he come here in Trouble, I better not write what way they went, nor his name neither, People might come and try to read my Book before I burn it, which I wouldn't like to do because it would be Stupid to do that to the Story of My Life if I don't have to, just to keep Information away from the Gunes. She says D himself says he'll be coming back.*

*He will too, wearing a rainbow, he'll make them look like Fools, drive them out of the Temple like it said in the Book—O how I go on! He was just my old Demetrios that was Janitor, never bothered nobody. Suppose it was on My Account he said he'd come back? He would always lean Way Over so not to hurt People when all the time he'd better of spoke Direct, not put everything like into a Story. Going off into the Fog and maybe not even enough to eat—well, that Garth is a good Boy, and maybe Solitaire got more ginger in her than I thought and won't be a Drag. Suppose I think about something else, like this Place for an Instance the way it was when I come from Raeford.*

112

*Not the coming here itself, that was mostly sickmaking, cars driv Crosswise onto the Road and People dead in them. My Trucker wasn't too bad, he said his name was Al, he'd been taking a ten-wheeler to New York with froze fish. He said everything on the Road went like crazy, maybe it was Blast, he run the ten-wheeler into an Embankment so not to hit a Lunatic in a Ford that come straight at him, and got hurt some in the Head, I mean my Trucker did, but got out and walked away from it, froze fish all over the Road. We was together a few days, walking west because he said he had people to Rochester and what's the difference, anything to be on the move. When he wanted it he would pull me down side of the Road and do it no matter somebody might go by, I didn't care either, I'd just keep still looking at the sky till he finished, all as he ever wanted was On and Off. He found food for me, and fought off a couple-three Gunes that wanted to Share the Wealth. In Beacon they shot him for looting. I crossed the River in a Motorboat with some Crazies that thought it was the Sea of Galilee and they'd see the Savior walking onto it, they wrecked the Boat landing in a Rainstorm and went off northways with their Ass dragging. I'd had it with them, up to here.*

*I say I won't write about a Thing, right off I go to doing it. Anyhow I come to Nuber chancelike, not caring. Already the Founders had got the Place in order, a regular Camp with Officers to tell People where to go, what to do. You can always feel the Difference when People got something to work on, not just flopping around like Crazies on the Sea of Galilee. Mister Fleur he was one of those Officers, working direct under Simon Bridgeman. I helped with refugees, the Hot Soup and Bandages bit, and in a couple-three months when Bridgeman's Government wanted to stablish some sex-houses, Mister Fleur's was the first.*

*Mister Fleur was kind to me, and a Friend too. He didn't want women but he liked them. Maybe it's easier to like them if you don't. He'd say things like it wasn't too bad of an Idear to have two Sexes because it made for interesting Arguments that People would never have* to settle because they couldn't. D sometimes talks kind of like Mister Fleur, account of Both was Educated.

Mister Fleur was a little sparrowy man, shorter than me but I had a great Respect for him, and he said I had a Good Business Head and a Sense of Order. Once-twice I've seen him pull the Switchblade he always carried to keep Peace in the House, but I never did see him obliged to use it, People got the Message right off and simmered down.

When Simon Bridgeman was murdered I thought it might have nearabout done for Mister Fleur. He was Tore Up. He might laugh some at Bridgeman's Idears, and criticize, but nobody else better, they was Friends and I guess he really thought S. Bridgeman was God, which I never noticed him thinking that about anybody else. He went on a two-week Drunk. Afterward he was like beat out, gone slack inside. He said the World wasn't worth a Packet of Shit—Present Company excepted of course, he was always Polite. Well, he straightened out after-while, but wasn't never again like when Bridgeman was living.

Sometimes he wanted to get me talking about the customers I'd serviced. He'd laugh, it would give him some kind of High, not the Thing itself but hearing me talk about it. I didn't mind.

It went on like that several years. Mister Fleur kept things Nice. People would come to us uptight—you'd be surprised how often the Yucks don't want to do nothing but talk and maybe collect some Sympathy about Things they can't change like wives and so forth and likely wouldn't if they could. They'd go away feeling better, anyhow quieter. Mister Fleur would say things like how Idealistic it was to work for a Public Utility that was actually in the Public Interest.

In Year 11 smallpox hit Nuber. I suppose somebody brang it in from Outside. Mister Fleur said all Bad Things come from Outside, the Inside is always Sinless like Desert Islands, I don't know all what he meant. Two of our girls died, and a Boy that Mister Fleur loved special come through the Sickness with his face looking for ever-after like a cheese-grater—and couldn't stand it

*neither but ran away from us, out of Nuber likely, for
Mister Fleur broke his heart trying to find him and never
could.*

*During that Smallpox he Also went around a lot help-
ing care for the sick, I guess he'd been a Doctor all right
in Old Time. But he never said so, and whenever he told
his name to anyone he'd pull himself up to his five foot
two and say, "I am Mis-ter Fleur," making the Mister
sound like ice tinging the edge of a glass.*

*After the Smallpox was over you could see how Old
Time pressed heavy on his Mind. And of course the Boy
Shawn, the one that run away. Mister Fleur didn't want
me to talk any more about the Customers, but he'd ask me
Things about Raeford, and Sam and Stevie and Leda,
sometimes about Marcus. He'd sit by me whiles I talked,
and pet me if I got to crying. Then one Night Mister Fleur
told me he'd fixed his Will so as I was to have the House
and the License if anything was to happen to him, all's
I had to do was go to the Town Hall, everything was on
Record, no Trouble, and he said he would Appreciate
it if I would keep the small room he slept in the way it
was, with the pictures Shawn painted, and never use it for
the Customers. Of course I said I would, and I always
have, sometimes I go there to just set and rest, only the
pictures are kind of Weird, there a'n't but two, I know
Shawn done others but must of flang them away. Well,
one shows the Holy Virgin only the Child is a Rag Doll,
and the other one is a great stud horse like climbing a
rainbow that Shawn painted him all purple and yellow,
you can't think how a Horse would get to look like That.
Once I showed Demetrios that room, and he said, "God
Almighty, Stell, what became of the Boy?" All's I could
tell him was, he went away, we couldn't ever find him.*

*So Mister Fleur said that about the Will, and then he
said I had a Good Head, and I wasn't to cry any more
about Marcus because that was the kind of cry that did
me no Good and I must make it like the Scar on my
Leg—well, you can't do that, but he meant it kind. He
went off to bed Peaceful, I remember, without no Drink
in him. Come morning we found he'd gone to bed per-*

*fectly natural and then rammed the Switchblade in under
his ribs.*

*He wasn't old, nor Sick or anything. I don't understand
how a Person could do that no matter how Things hurt—
I suppose it gets to be like not caring, maybe, but wouldn't
they always want to know what happens Next?*

All day the wood-road led the Company south and
southwest, in a prodigious quiet for which Demetrios's
ears were not ready. At Nuber, even in the slack dead of
night, one heard at least a contracting of house timbers,
rustle of mice, drop of spent coals in a fireplace, dog or
cat noises, a murmur, a footstep; by day the continual
street sounds—wagon wheels, clop of hoofs, bray of don-
keys, peddlers' cries. Here, not even wind. All day the
fog never truly lifted, merely thinning to admit watery
light and a sufficient view of the road. At the noontime
halt—the Company sensed rather than saw that the sun
was overhead—Demetrios asked Bosco if wilderness always imposed this quiet. "My ignorance shames me,"
Demetrios said. "No wilderness existed in Old Time except very far from the places I knew, and then I was
spending all my time in Nuber, that hothouse, while wilderness grew back around us and all I knew of it was folk-
say."

"Where there's a road," said Bosco, "even a wispy one
like this, it a'n't wilderness exactly. Real wilderness, you
work from tree to tree, and remember your back trail.
Some kinds of jungle, like western Moha near the On-
tara, you got to cut your way. I don't understand this
road myself. Never seen a woods road go this long without
getting no place. Nor like you say, this quiet. There'd
ought to be animal sounds, not just them birds now and
then. I believe it's the fog, and the 'umidity. Our sweat
smells, see, and the critters catch it and keep still. Like
everything was afraid of man, a'n't it strange?"

"Funny deer-tracks back-along," said Frankie.

Bosco tolerantly regarded him and his brother. "Wa'n't
deer-tracks, Frankie. Them was boar, and a big feller." Sitting weary between Angus and the Professor, Solitaire
shivered; she could not have done this much walking in

116

a whole day since the time when Demetrios found her, and her first enthusiasm had dimmed in fatigue; Bosco saw it. "Not to worrit," he said. "Boar a'n't likely to bother you unless he thinks you're hunting him, or you go crashing into some place he figures is his'n. Besides, them sign was made yesterday."

Angus nodded, watching her. "Brand wasn't interested. He would have been hot for work if the smell had been fresh, in spite of picking up that rabbit for breakfast this morning."

"The little thing." Yet Solitaire's hand moved in affection over Brand's ferocious head.

"He must kill to live," said Angus, in futile distress because the world could not harmonize with what he saw of this woman's nature.

"Solitaire knows that," she said. "People too. Meat is good. Beasts all, all beasts," said Solitaire; and hearing her small, disturbed laugh, Demetrios dreaded the next moments, for she would be weeping uncontrollably, almost silently, her hands palms upward in her lap as if waiting for alms that no one knew how to give.

The Professor heard that laugh too, and before the flood of tears began he took her lightly in his arms as anyone might take a child in trouble. Angus stared at Demetrios in amazed distress. But words could not be used while her trouble was on her, and if he went aside with Angus to explain how this would pass, how it was a thing one accepted if one accepted Solitaire, she would see them go, and a rage might follow. For she had her rages too, though no one was ever hurt by them except in spirit: would Angus still worship after witnessing one of those?

Garth and Bosco were looking away in heavy embarrassment, but Frankie, after his first moment of alarm, searched rapidly in his hip satchel. He brought out a fragment of admirable carving—it was apple-wood, Demetrios thought. A fawn lay curled like a sleeping kitten but with open eyes. The treasure was no bigger than that Japanese netsuke of a laughing old woman which had been one of the marvels on the desk of Dr. Isaac Freeman, very long since. Frankie laid the fawn on Solitaire's open palm. "Garth done it," he said. "You might like to look at it. I a'n't no good at them things myself."

The tears stopped, the fingers closed. "Frankie—O the eyes of him!"

"You can keep it if you want," said Frankie. "I got about a thousand more. He does 'em all the time, my brother does. . . ."

In the early evening the Company reached a spot where the wood-road touched the remnant of an Old-Time paved surface, the kind the ancients called blacktop. Dimly beyond the junction the wood-road continued. The Old-Time road was so desolate, so far from any sense of intelligent creation, it seemed less like evidence of humanity than the trail they had been following. On that they could at least find, though intermittently, the dint of wagon-wheels gone by a week or two before, but the Old-Time road offered no more than a long vanishing aisle under dense growth, a surface of black dull patches nearly hidden by grass and weeds that had pressed through tiny cracks, started by frost or earthquake or time, and made them big. Here and there seedling trees were pushing into light; these in a few more years would do away with even the memory of the road. And nowhere in the green cover could the Company find any human mark. Animals would have been crossing it repeatedly, the grass springing up behind them, but had formed no visible trails down the length of it; possibly any human creatures who looked along the desolate way would have chilled themselves with the thought of ghosts and wanted no part of it. But Angus said: "I have in my head a sort of compass. I think it speaks true mostly. Spin me around, I still know somehow where the west is, if there's any daylight or moonlight—it doesn't help me in real darkness. I used to astonish my family with it when I was a boy. Well, my compass says this wood-road has been trending a little bit east for the last hour, as if it meant to angle back toward the Great South Road where we daren't show our faces. But the Old-Time thing is pointing clear west." He shook his dark hair behind his shoulder; one of his

118

rare smiles touched Demetrios. "I smell the Pacific in front of my nose, three thousand miles away."

Maybe, thought Demetrios, that was how it would be for all of the journey, and how it ought to be: Angus, the wisest of the young, would be the true maker of decisions and giver of directions, but he would employ his uncanny tact and he would seek the old man's counsel. Under such conditions, possibly a little democracy of seven souls could be made to function without doing too much violence to seven patterns of need. A democracy of seven plus Brand, who might take occasion to vote now and then after his fashion.

*(This was probably the moment, your novelist supposes, when Demetrios-sacred-to-the-Earth decided to found his own republic, if he could keep it. A republic needs mothers to breed its sons and daughters. He knew that.)*

The Company covered better than a mile of the Old-Time road, finding no change in its quality, and camped comfortably beside it before dark. It seemed safe to build a good fire. In this quiet and loneliness—the fog was with them still, faint in the air but sad like all memories of antiquity—the thought of pursuit from Nuber appeared ridiculous, even to Angus. "The powers of Inner City," he said, "have nothing against me except my existence. They are rewriting history, by the way, did I tell you? My uncle Simon may have to appear as an arch-villain, Antichrist, whatever, instead of a saint. Saints can be a mite inconvenient to a King's Republic—sooner or later some crackpot is going to insist on imitating them, and that means more damn work for the cops." He laid gently on the little furnace of the fire the stick he had been using to stir it up. "My disappearance ought to suit them almost as well as—say, a sudden fatal illness or a stiletto in the back. Of course it may worry them a bit, can't help that."

"Will Angus go back there sometime?"

He gazed at Solitaire a long time across the fire. "Nay, I think not. Vengeance is nothing but a sickness, and what other reason would I have? To save the Abramites from persecution?—they are already under the wheels, and I have no power."

"One day," said Demetrios, "the Abramites will themselves be the oppressors. An old rhythm of history, another punishment by nature of those who were too busy rewriting history to read it."

"I think I understand you," said Angus. "No—no, I won't go back." He leaned toward the fire, seeking to bring her face nearer to his eyes. "I've no wish for any place where you couldn't safely come with me." From his quiet speech no one could have said whether "you" meant only Solitaire or all the Company; but the Professor's lute broke out in a sudden music, and Frankie came quickly around the fire to kneel by him and watch his sovereign fingers on the strings. They were carrying a familiar melody in and out of shadows, letting it play beatific games with itself. On the exact moment, as the Professor nodded to him, Frankie sang, shy at first but then with the assurance of an angel, the air, said to have been composed by a streetcorner musician of Brakabin in recent years, his name no more known than the name of Demetrios, certainly not a music of Old Time:

> Before the dark falls
> your flesh is amber fire
> to warm my midnight.
>
> Before a light spreads
> your mouth gives solace of night
> to cool my noontime.
>
> I have not wondered
> that flame and coolness perish:
> to love is mortal.

## CHAPTER ELEVEN

### *They noticed a Sign saying DEAD END*

> *. . . But we had enemies which he called magicians,
> and they had turned the whole thing into an infant
> Sunday-school just out of spite. I said, all right; then
> the thing for us to do was to go for the magicians.
> Tom Sawyer said I was a numbskull.*
> — *Mark Twain, THE ADVENTURES
> OF HUCKLEBERRY FINN.*

All of the next day, and the next, the ruined road led
the Company west and a little south. The fog was a burden, full of sounds. It seemed to Demetrios that he was
hearing out of the mist what could never be heard again,
absurd with antiquity. Wasn't that a police siren beyond
fog-shrouded trees?—not the full scream but the yow-
yow-yow patrol cars used to make to clear traffic out of
their way? "Durn parrots," said Bosco. "Them little whitey
ones."

"Ayah," said Angus. "My mother keeps one in a cage."

An hour later the siren made its other fearful cry, the
one for accident, disaster, fire. "Durn-by-damn," said
Bosco. "Don't often hear catamount sound off like that in
the daytime."

"Overcast days," said Garth. "Or if he's horny."

"I heard one last night," said Frankie. "Same, likely."

Demetrios could accept it. When in time another shrill-
ness sounded, faint and small with distance, he could scold
himself for hearing the noon whistle of a factory or town
siren. But he asked the boy with the Old-Time wristwatch:
"What's the time, Angus?"

"Noon straight up, man Demetrios."

Auto horns—the afternoon in mid-flight—auto horns—anyway a confused hooting or bleating. Was the mist itself generating this madness? It had seemed in the last half-hour to be lifting. Now and then Demetrios had glimpsed the sun's white blur, finding it too strong to look on directly. Moose or deer trumpeting? A daytime owl? He saw Garth frown and Frankie look at him with inquiry, but no one spoke of it, and presently it ceased.

They noticed a sign saying DEAD END.

"Crossroads, huh?" said Bosco.

"God," said Garth, "I wish I could read."

Bosco caught Demetrios's eye. "I don't know as that's what it says, but you can see another road coming in here, north and south."

The placard was of ancient metal, raised letters partly obliterated. Beyond it the black patches and disorderly green cover of the Old-Time road continued. Brand sniffed at the sign and raised his leg. "Sure I'll teach you and Frankie to read," said Angus. "Or Demetrios will, or both of us."

"Solitaire can teach some," said the frail pregnant lady. "Solitaire had the books a little, once."

"Books makes folk discontented," said Bosco.

"I don't mind discontent," said Demetrios. Bosco shrugged, amiable, finding it not worth an argument. "Let's go on west. If it's really a dead end we can turn back."

The old blacktop went on more firmly if anything. Perhaps someone had played a joke, long forgotten; or the road had been extended after the sign was placed; or whoever was carrying the sign got sick of it and rammed it in the ground just there—it's a crazy world. When later the Company began to hear a vague roaring, felt in the feet and knees and guts, Demetrios refused to think of heavy trucks pelting down a highway through air blue with poison to feed a monstrous city. "Must be a real old man of a waterfall somewhere," said Bosco.

The road was veering slightly south. The noise diminished. When it came time to camp for the night they still felt its booming in the ground but hardly thought about it.

*Once long ago, a day or two before Aberedo, I dreamed*

*my father was living, and it dismayed my witless dream-self though I had loved him, though we were friends in an easier, kindlier way than son and father ordinarily can be, because he was not vain. If with a wand or a prayer I could make Old Time return, what would I do? . . .*

Demetrios also brooded on his memory of Old-Time maps. They could meet no great river before the Delaware. Were they already approaching it? The sound droned on, chaos talking in its sleep.

Angus was taking the first two-hour watch. Garth with Frankie would have the next, then Bosco; Demetrios with the Professor would take the last, that led into dawn. Demetrios sought his blanket but feared sleep—he did not wish to dream of Hesterville. On the other side of the fire Solitaire and the Professor sat talking. Her lips moved, close to his ear; his face expressed innumerable changes of doubt, assent, agreement, brooding. He had put away his lute. He seldom made explanatory motions of his hands, but his fingers often danced on the bridge of his right arm, and Solitaire watched that. *Ah, Paisan! Maybe you don't speak because you don't want to. If voices reach you, if a certain few love you and discover your answers, it is enough?*

The dark was lightened by a blurred moon; overhead Vega, a few other eternal lights. A transitory music disturbed Demetrios, appallingly like the noise made by the radio of a quiet car driving by in the distance; he heard or imagined muted motor noise, passage of tires along damp pavement. It happened again. He could see now, in the night depth, part of the configuration of the Great Bear. The mist was surely dissolving under a breeze; he saw the wavering of the black lacework of summer branches. So, in among them the wind rubbed a few to-gether and whined its musical breath across them. . . . Solitaire was kneeling by him. "Angus spread his blanket by the spruce tree," she said, "before he went on watch."

"Yes." Her hand was soft, a little heavy on his arm.

"Nothing comes between Demetrios and Solitaire."

"Nothing."

"Paisan knows too. It's a need."

"Understood."

123

"Angus is gentle. The child will be safe under his loving."

"Go to him. This isn't Old Time."

"What about Old Time, man Demetrios?"

"Ah, nothing. Go to him, love." He had not been certain until then that his love for Angus was firm enough to let him say it. Old mythologies die painfully; but she would understand in her own fashion: there was no measuring the strength or direction of her wisdom which was so much like her madness (said Mam Estelle once) that it was silly to draw lines between them.

Perhaps the blue ice of Vega was not quite clear of mist. He heard and felt the waterfall, continuing not forever, only till the next earthquake, next shift of climate in the four-billion-year time clock—or whatever the estimate was when science ceased to be heard. He roused heavily from sleep. Bosco was refreshing the fire with new wood. "Is it my watch?"

"Nay, only midnight. I'm going on. Sorry I disturbed you."

"No matter. All quiet?"

"Quiet enough. Garth and Frankie heard a wolf—wa'n't close by. Might've been just k'yote-dog, Garth says."

"Too deep for that," said Frankie, and he spread his blanket by Demetrios. "It were a wolf, by lone."

"A'n't he a pisser? Now if he was my little brother—"

"Think what I missed!" Frankie chirped, and settled himself for slumber, Garth rolled up on his other side; but Frankie was restless, and soon whispered: "Demetrios, be you much asleep? Would I talk you into telling me a story?"

"Don't bother the man," Garth yawned.

"I'm not bothered." Demetrios sat up in his blanket. The night held an unseasonable forest chill, and his bones were aching, not adapting well to sleeping on the ground. "You might, Frankie. It's only the truth there was a young painter in the old days of Peranelios, marvelous skillful, though I can't tell you whether he became famous, in spite of the fact that I know everything. His name was Mister Jon and he wished to paint heroes."

"Is painting like singing?"

124

"Somewhat yes, someway no." He drew Frankie into the hollow of his arm: his left hand fed the fire with little twigs: warmth quieted pain. "More like than unlike, and storytelling is like both. Mister Jon (who wasn't much older than you) had no ambition except to be the greatest painter who ever lived. He consulted Bald Ape-Man (the most respected critic in Peranelios) about this, and Bald Ape-Man asked him: 'Do you want to be the greatest painter who ever lived, or do you want to paint?' Being in a sense the brains of the outfit, Mister Jon got the point, and set before Bald Ape-Man a nice ripe melon he had brought, to acknowledge the fact that he had so much more sense than most critics. You always bring something if you consult him; a lot depends on whether he eats it or throws it at you. Then Mister—"

"Well, which?"

"Which what?"

"Did he eat it or throw it at him?"

"Oh. Some say one, some say another—the kind of thing a storyteller runs into constantly. Mister Jon, as I said, wished to paint heroes because he thought they were interesting, I don't know why exactly, but in Peranelios, same as anywhere, the problem is to find them."

"Where's Peranelios?"

"Other side of the Never-Today Mountains."

"I thought prob'ly. Like the fairy tales my aunt tells, things always happen where you can't go. But," said Frankie, warm and drowsy. "I'd rather listen to one anytime than go to sleep. Anytime."

"So would I. Mister Jon asked his father if he knew where to find any heroes. Mister Jon's father had fought in the wars against the pirates, was in fact aboard the flagship when the fleet crept before dawn through the Narrows of Gor to attack the pirates' secret harbor. He had no idea where Mister Jon could find any heroes, and was cross with him for interrupting a glass of beer. Mister Jon drew a sketch of him looking cross, and left home that night to look for heroes. The picture bothered him by looking more like himself than like his father, but much later, when he was hard up, he managed to sell it to an admiral who had known his father, for the price of a night's lodging and a bowl of soup.

"On his first day away from home he came on a brawny young armored horseman with a lance confronting a fearsome fiery dragon, which was just what he was looking for. He asked the noble youth: 'Would you just hold that lance a mite more slantwise?—okay, that's it. By the way, aren't you fighting over something, maiden or whatever?'

" 'Well, we sent for her,' said the dragon, 'but the little misery is late. She always is.'

" 'Dunno what gets into maidens nowadays,' said the hero, who was older than Mister Jon had thought. 'They aren't what they were. Let's not wait. Have I got this right, with the lance?'

" 'Fine,' said Mister Jon.

" 'My other profile is better,' said the dragon. They fixed that, and it turned out to be his most salable painting—he did several, with improvements and maidens and so on—but Mister Jon wasn't satisfied: the hero, and sometimes the dragon, always looked like himself. He hunted up other types of hero, and had the same difficulty. The subjects couldn't see it—they were looking of course only for their own selves and (of course) always found them—but Mister Jon saw it. It still bothered him when he arrived at the capital.

"There he consulted the Great Stone Face, which stands in a fine plaza in the capital of Peranelios and is the *twice*-as-much respected critic in the whole nation, since it never says anything at all. Its manner of never saying anything conveyed to Mister Jon that the hero thing itself might be causing the trouble. Instead of heroes perhaps he ought to paint only the most noble, brave, and beatific people he could find, He tried that, earning somewhat less than before, though a number of nice people had nice things to say. You see, the trouble was—the trouble was—"

"They all looked like him," said Frankie. "But the people he painted couldn't see it, right?"

"Right. He could. After a while he found out why it was."

"Guess you better tell me."

126

"He himself was the only person of any kind he actually knew. He could love others, and paint them, but never know. He was hero, thief, beggar, dragon, saint. I forgot to tell you his last name was Everyman. Mister Jon Everyman."

"I guess it's a sort of a sad story." Frankie yawned.

"I guess. Might not be all that sad after a good sleep."

"Might not." Frankie burrowed back into his blanket, where presently a large sigh tapered off into a small snore.

*My novelist's privilege is to say that as he sat on there by the fire feeding it little twigs, until Bosco came to give him the wristwatch for his tour of guard duty with the Professor, Demetrios composed other endings for that story, some of which might be more suited to Frankie's youth. How superior we do feel! Maturity ought to mean more than just knowing a bunch of shit the kids haven't caught onto yet, but how often does it?) I could give you a few, but you'd get impatient. Not that I'd blame you— here we are in Chapter Eleven and still in the fog along with Huck Finn, Dante, all that lot.*

In the morning the mist had grown deep once more, and it was under the mist that the Company found the old road improving, becoming a decent small thoroughfare. Grass and weeds were beaten down though not destroyed, the more threatening saplings had been chopped off— road work, for which we may hope somebody got paid. The noise of waterfall diminished, subtly changed, as the Company moved on west: it was more like the protest of a river forced between narrow banks, and Demetrios could feel it as deeply as ever, a vibration in the ground.

Another crossroad angled in; half a mile further on, another, from the south. Along this, looming big and blurred in the mist, then sharpening to natural outlines, came a graying couple with a golden bird in a cage. They nodded politely to the Company, and the man asked: "Be you on your way to the ferry?"

"If that's where the road goes," said Demetrios—for this morning Angus, drowsy and absent-minded from a night of tender games, appeared to want Demetrios to be leader and decision maker.

The stranger woman didn't like that answer. "Where

else would it go?" she demanded, and she may have thought Demetrios or her husband deaf, for she repeated: "I say where else could it go?" Her man carrying the cage—they had no other baggage—smiled placatingly.

Solitaire left her place by Angus and chirped her lips at the bird, who broke into wild caroling under her gaze. "Give him here," said the woman, "I say, give him here." She took the cage—no doubt the man really was deaf—and covered it with a gray cloth she had been carrying tucked under her belt. The singing ceased. "We'll walk a ways behind you good folk," she said. "That way he won't make so much trouble."

Frankie fell back presently to make friends with them, but they were embarrassed or afraid (was it possible to be afraid of Frankie? yes)—covering the bird again hastily because its music burst forth at his mere approach. Demetrios glimpsed his efforts, which won only tight-mouth mumbles from the woman, dim smiles from the man. Soon Frankie gave it up and rejoined the Company, baffled and rather angry; but whatever he said was for Garth's ears only. The couple plodded on ten yards or so behind, and no one else had turned up when they all came down a long stony slope to the ferry-house.

It stood between fog-laced trees. Fog held the waters beyond it to infinity. The Company was hardly aware of the presence of the stream until they had reached the ferry-house itself; then here, magnified by the high bank, the slow great noise of it was all around them. As on the previous days, the fog appeared to be thinning off, yet never did, quite; or if it did, this was no more than the tantalizing lift of a curtain which for clumsy reasons of its own must come down one more time—

*If you ever got stuck with a part in amateur theatricals (which haven't improved noticeably since the original carry-on among the Swiss lake-dwellers) you'll have noticed the mess we invariably run into with the damned curtain—sticks, comes down too soon on the tenor's neck, works any way except right—if there's a curtain at all; some try to get along without one, try to smuggle the cast in behind a screen till called for, and the fat one drops his spear, clank, clongle, and when he stoops for it his ass*

128

*knocks the screen over and there they be (the Swiss lake-
dwellers always used a curtain) what I'm wishing to con-
vey is that if you've had this Experience it just might give
you some sympathy with a novelist obliged to deal with
the fog and stuff in this chapter (I won't even have time
for Mam Estelle) when it would be so much simpler and
safer to trot along with the nice swift-paced action story
you thought, dear soul, you were going to get for sure
this time—what a pity*

The ferry-house stood gray and old, the pier worn with
traffic (yet no one else was coming now) and green in its
sheltered parts with water-weed and mold. The furled sail
of the ferry dripped condensing fog. But a cheerful lamp
was visible through the inshore window of the ferry-house.
The Manager could be seen sopping up a lunch of fried
egg with a piece of bread, wiping a gray moustache. His
name appeared on a sign above the door:

DELAWARE CROSSING
(Washinton Slep here)
R.C.Noah, Mgr.
CUSTOM SAILINGS 10¢

Mr. Noah flung wide the door before they could enter,
a gray titan dwarfing Bosco's mass and Demetrios's height.
Brand cringed as Demetrios had never yet seen him do,
recovering his courage swiftly but making no overtures
of friendship though Mr. Noah was beaming after his grim
fashion. "So wha'd'y' want?" He was just a big, rude, noisy
old man in a gray loincloth, with egg smears on his mus-
tache.

"We're traveling west," said Angus. "When's your next
trip?"

"Any time. I don't run no goddamn timetable. What's
nice people like you want to go west for?"

"I came from there," said Demetrios.

"That's no reason. Nothing now except wilderness, after Penn."

"We don't like it where we are," said Bosco. "See? By
the way, Mister, you seen or heard anything of an outfit
called Gammo's Ramblers?"

"No."

"We're separate," said the woman with the bird cage. "Here, take it while I get out the change." But she had to shake her husband's arm to get his attention. "I say, take the cage while I get out the change."

"Needn't to be in no such rush, ma'am," said Mr. Noah. "We ain't gosemplacing no place till I been to the john and back."

"Disgusting fellow!" But she said that under her breath, and after Mr. Noah had ducked back into his diminutive ferry-house.

"He ain't so long on politeness, it's a fact," said Bosco. "All's I done was ask a fair question." Solitaire too had shown a flare of anger, but at the touch of Angus's arm around her she relaxed, looking up at him in a haze of confidence. Bosco added: "Y' know, I ain't sure I could take that guy."

Frankie laughed. Demetrios said: "Don't try, man." Frankie ceased laughing and moved nearer to Garth, who was at that moment the calmest of the Company.

Mr. Noah returned and strode down the narrow wharf, blocking access to his miserable boat by standing there with an open palm. The stranger woman moved in ahead, glaring at Angus though he had already stepped back for her. She placed a dime in Mr. Noah's hand. "We only got half of your outrageous fare. Supposed to be a nickel."

"For half I can take you halfway across," said Mr. Noah.

"I never heard such nonsense!"

"Or I'll take the bird in pay for the other half. Nice little bird like that would brighten up the joint."

"Well—all right. Give him the cage." Her husband smiled on gently into the fog. "I say, give him the cage." She snatched it from him herself and gave it to Mr. Noah, who lifted away the cloth.

The bird cocked an eye at Mr. Noah and tenderly sang. "There!" said Mr. Noah. "There now!" He was still admiring his acquisition when Angus paid, but was attentive enough to notice the eight dimes. He gave one back. "Won't charge the dog nothing. He kills a rat or two it'll more'n pay his fare." Demetrios saw a red-gray slick-moving shape scuttle under a thwart as the stranger couple stumbled forward in the boat looking for the driest place to sit. "Be he a good ratter? The rats is awful lately."

"Oh, he's death on rats," said Angus.

"By God I could do with a good ratter around the place."

"I could never sell him."

"Didn't much think you would. He can still ride for free." They got no more conversation from Mr. Noah. He spread the soggy sail, pushed off, took the tiller, and whistled up a breeze—well, it had actually begun to blow, and favorably, about five minutes before he whistled, thinning out the fog into lazy-floating ghosts and spirits of sadness that made way for the advancing sail above gray water—

*—for there was always plenty of ham in Mr. Noah, otherwise the Delaware Crossing Corporation could hardly have kept him in that job as long as they have, and if he chose to make it appear that a minor shift of surface meteorological conditions came about in response to his whistle, his personal egg-eating will, I suppose he can be allowed that little vanity; especially since I am almost done with this part of the book, the fog part. On the whole you've been very patient, very nice. Thank you.*

Brand did kill that rat, and the golden bird did sing— vigorously, after the sun came through enough to show evergreens and willows on the approaching bank. A great river, though not the widest; the shore the travelers had left behind was not visible when they disembarked, but that was because of the fog lingering over there, evidently characteristic of this part of the world. The Company watched Mr. Noah reentering that fog-bank; Demetrios thought he heard the golden bird still singing.

Beyond the landing the Old-Time road continued, in better repair. No more fog. Every branch, every little stone and weed was washed in the clean warmth of afternoon. At the first crossroad the stranger woman said: "We go this way." She tugged at her husband's arm. He nodded diffidently to Demetrios; they were gone.

The Company had moved on a quarter of a mile, each heart following its own course in solitude, when Solitaire

131

stopped in her tracks, eyes dilated. She had been walking with Angus, lovingly though without touching him. She swung about and ran back down the road a short way, and hurled her oaken stick savagely in the direction the stranger couple had taken. *"Fools! Idiots!"* She tried to shout more, but it strangled on the weeping in her throat.

Demetrios reached her first and held her lightly; sometimes in her rages she had torn her clothes, raked her arms with her nails. He felt her shrink, and again when Angus took her hands, but she made no effort to break free. "What if the bird dies?"

"I suppose," said Angus, "some would say he was their bird."

"He was. But he sang for Solitaire. He sang for Frankie."

"Solitaire—"

"What do you mean? Who is Solitaire? O Demetrios, Demetrios, what if Solitaire lost her madness? What could Solitaire do without her madness? There wasn't any gang-rape, Demetrios. Why—why, she just strayed from Brakabin, got lost, the stupid thing, all the way from Brakabin because her stupid damn mother told her to walk the stupid damn dog, she would have had to go past the house where my—my—the house where my—"

She watched her tight hands relax as Angus rubbed them. He said: "The bird was singing when the ferryman sailed with him."

She nodded and smiled, brilliantly, rationally. But memory closed the door that some passion had briefly blown open. That was all the Company ever did learn of whatever world had made Solitaire whatever she was. Frankie recovered the oak branch and she accepted it. "O Brains of the Outfit," she said, "we start learning letters at the next halt, and it won't be easy."

"So what's easy?"

"That's my friend. Now Solitaire wants music."

As they walked on she swung her stick in rhythm with the old man's, having linked arms with Demetrios as a free and independent spirit, and the Professor fell in behind them plinking a sassy march. Frankie darted in before them as a drum major, beating on the tin dish from his sack with his pewter spoon, and caroling ancient and venerable words in response to the Professor's tune:

"Mademoiselle from Armentières, parlez-vous?
Mademoiselle from Armentières, parlez-vous—
She's hard to curry above the knees
But falls on her back with the greatest of ease.
Hinky-dinky, parlez-vous!"

(Some verses have survived that even Frankie didn't know.) Garth whistled and sang a bit himself. Angus blasted away at a grass-blade set between his thumbs. Bosco pounded his chest and slapped his thighs, now and then going *boom!* for a bass drum, and Brand frisked about in astonished admiration, making dog noises off pitch. Thus it was that the Company came down in fine though informal style on the peaceable, prosperous, somewhat conservative Penn town of Trottersville.

The Old-Time road had petered out; through the trees could be seen a better, modern dirt road, with reasonable hoofprints, sandal-marks, wagon tracks. As *Mademoiselle* brought them out on this they saw, quite near, rooftops on lower ground, pasture fences, a church spire catching sunlight. Demetrios described for Angus the spectacle of men and dogs driving a herd of shoats down to the village, on the other side of town where a low hill lifted the road. Trottersville was a pigs and chickens town. A rooster crowed. Bosco smiled.

Trottersville, as everyone knows, was founded ages ago by a family named Trotter (or Trotters), but the only statue on the green is that of a pig, done in one of the late 20th Century styles to look like an egg-beater except from the south. The inscription in the pedestal reads MY THING, but this has been filled with putty and painted, so maybe it shouldn't be discussed, though it does keep showing through. From the south The Little Hog looks more like a pair of scissors upside down. Every weather-vane in town is a gilded cock.

The Company made for the inn, Angus confident of the value of his Katskil money. The hostel displayed a sign of a boar's head, and carried medieval tradition further by

133

placing an evergreen branch to project from the doorway and tell the illiterate that drinks were to be had here. Angus's money was good indeed, the loft was available with room for everyone including Brand, and the drinks were drinkable.

Best of all, Sawyer Finn's Circus was in town.

# CHAPTER TWELVE

## *It's our Covenant with Nature*

> *Wynken, Blynken, and Nod one night*
> *Sailed off in a wooden shoe—*
> *Sailed on a river of crystal light*
> *Into a sea of dew.*
>     *—Eugene Field,*
>      *POEMS OF CHILDHOOD.*

The innkeeper at the Boar's Head, ancient and knowledgeable, surely a survivor of Old Time, thought he might have heard of Gammo's Ramblers a few years ago—couldn't place it. "They might know up at the Circus—those old crackpots get around. Jason Smallways has lent 'em his back field to camp in. Show opens tomorrow—no tent, just the caravans and freaks and whatnot."

"I'll ask," Bosco said. "Anybody want to come along?"

"I will," said Demetrios. "Sawyer Finn's, did you say?"

The innkeeper confirmed it. "T.S. and H.F. they call themselves. Old nuts that got cracked—maybe that's who they really think they are. But I shouldn't talk, sir—I get notional myself."

Frankie and the Professor joined them; the rest were tired, or sad, or busy. They passed through the drowsy town—all Penn is drowsy, it's partly the climate—to the animal-smelling excitement in Smallways' back forty. Mule-caravans were drawn up in a loose ring, almost like Conestoga wagons surrounded by war-whoops. An acrobat tried the stretch of his tights lately mended in the seat. A boy exercised two pretty horses. An old square-jawed gentleman tested a ringmaster's whip, snapping it at the ground, and a scrawny man with black mustaches petted

135

two pumas in a cage. A fat woman sat in the sun, grieving and still.

The old gentleman eyed them uneasily, as Bosco went to talk with the horse-boy. "Another committee bound to civilize us! I never see such a power of committees." But he was not unfriendly.

"I never civilized anybody," said Demetrios.

"Now I look at you, I reckon you never did. Who's the boy?"

"I'm Frankie, and this is the Professor. He doesn't talk, but Miz Solitaire is teaching me to tell what he thinks."

The old man nodded. "Looking for a job, any of you?"

"Depends," said Demetrios. "We're heading west."

"Be you the big boss?"

"Naw, Frankie, I'm Vice-President. Just H.F." He called to one of the caravans. "O T.S.! Mister Vice-President! Company!" The Professor's lute asked a question. "Oh, he's the *other* Vice-President." The lute inquired one thing more. "President? Why, how you talk! Wouldn't have one on the place. You T.S.! . . . You know, it ain't no use going west. Ocean, jungle, islands.⁻ The map ain't what it was—you could throw a dog through it anywheres." He shucked his frock coat, wiping off sweat. "I got to wear this at the opening tomorrow—for style, T.S. says—but no use killing myself." His blue jeans, like those Frankie and Demetrios wore, had patches at knees and rear. *"Mister Vice-President!* What's gone with that man, I wonder? Sleeps later every afternoon."

Two midgets appeared, man and woman, with another woman close to normal size, about four feet ten. The midgets were in faultless proportion, the dark-haired man three feet tall. The red-haired, blue-eyed women bore a facial resemblance affirming sisterhood. The man spoke in a voice of alto pitch: "T.S. isn't asleep. His sore toe's bothering him, but he said he'd be along." He bowed in the stage manner, not in mockery but as if he enjoyed it: "I am Nod, Minuscule Marvel of the Modern Mundane Masque. I have the honor to present my wife Wynken, and my wife Blynken."

"I'm Blynken," said the taller woman. She dimpled,

136

shaking hands. "Marriage is such a convenience, now and then!"

"I'm Wynken." Wynken's eyes were nearer soft green than blue.

"We were the Cabot sisters of Lowelltown before we married—originally Kabotski of course—perhaps you're not from Massachusetts—"

"Stuff it, Blynk," said Wynken. "These are friends."

The other Vice-President emerged at last, in his own frock coat. He wore a dainty felt hat too, perhaps only for the sake of lifting it expressively. He was all courtesy, thus reminding Demetrios in no way of the 20th Century. "I don't know what H.F. is thinking of to let you stand out here in the sun. Do come into the caravan."

Nod said: "I thought I'd go over with—"

"Blynken to look at the horses," said Blynken, "while—"

"Wynken's always crazy about strangers," said Wynken.

"Consound it," said H.F., "they do that all the time. It's like talking to somebody with three heads."

"There's a trick to it," said Wynken, and she reached her hand up to H.F.'s as they walked to the caravan. Studying the new faces, she swished her long skirt and hummed to herself:

> " 'We have come to fish for the herring fish
>     That live in the beautiful sea;
>     Nets of silver and gold have we!'
>         Said Wynken,
>         Blynken,
>         And Nod."

Both old men were white-haired, carved with wrinkles, eyes a little blurred at the iris. They moved carefully on thin legs (T.S. gave no sign of martyrdom to a sore toe) but they did not stoop; they were clear-voiced, pink-cheeked. They graciously indicated which parts of the caravan floor were best to sit on. "We are embarrassed for furniture," said T.S., "a bucolic sheriff having attached some of our choicest pieces, including a rocking chair to which I was much attached. It belonged at one time to my aunt. Of course it's only a temporary inconvenience."

137

Wynken had served a round of corn spirit in little chipped cups. "Allow me, my dear—" T.S. flicked a handkerchief over the floor where she was about to sit.

Frankie nosed around like a cat in a new house, but he was already in love, obliged to sit down as far as possible from Wynken and become somewhat red and bug-eyed.

"Better times are coming," said T.S. "Something is bound to turn up. It always does. Where are you from, sir?"

Demetrios told the story of Nuber. Sawyer Finn's Circus had never visited there, though Wynken said she and her sister and their husband knew something of it from earlier years. And Demetrios told of Hesterville, of a culture that had died partly from self-hate. T.S. said: "Yes—yes—we hoped it wouldn't happen . . ."

"What would you think of going back west, Mister Vice?"

"Oh, I'm afraid we can't, Mister Veep. All changed— we wouldn't know those islands. No public for a circus so far as I can see, and we do have to make a living, H.F."

"That lute would sure give the Circus a tone," said H.F.

"The Professor," said Frankie (showing off some), "is thinking he'll always go wherever we go." The lute agreed. Then Frankie yielded to inexorable forces and spoke directly to Wynken, forsaking all others: "How old be you?"

"I am as young as I am old, Frankie, love."

"I guess that's all right." He studied his desperate toes. "Only I wish you was coming with us."

The lute spoke in the silence; Wynken was listening. She looked in disturbance to Demetrios, who smiled at her. By his guess she could have been anywhere between twenty and thirty-five; midgets are uncanny. "T.S.," she said, "Blynken and Nod and I have been talking lately about something that bugs us, only I wasn't ready to speak up. It's been on our minds—oh, ever since those yucks almost egged us back there at Betlam—"

"Cruds, every one." But T.S. knew what was coming.

"T.S., darling, we aren't lucky for the show and you know it."

"Land of Goshen, child! Nonsense!" It did not ring true.

"T.S., we *can't* do much except flutter around and be small. And the yucks—oh—Blynken says she's losing her knack with the fortune-telling—it never was her thing anyway. If she could be in our act—but she's too big. Nod and I—oh, we dance, and we're good with the horses because they like us. But it doesn't go over. The yucks want us to be freaks. Oh, it was fairly tough when we were living in the woods, and you were angels to get us out of that, but—T.S., H.F., the yucks want to despise us. They want to think how wonderful it is of them, not to be little people. If we could be awkward or ugly they'd like us well enough."

"Sho!" said H.F. "That *can't* be, honey." But he must have known it was so. "What'd we do without you, Mary Ja—Wynken?"

"Oh . . . We'll put on a good show tomorrow. Don't worry. We'll sleep on it, talk again. I—" Wynken ran out of the caravan. Glancing back at Frankie. Chickened out, you might say.

[Friday, July 26]

*What for do we try so hard to entertain people? There's two ways. For Money, like this House, where they come in uptight and we send them out pacified, almost like Sensible—like when my old Demetrios used to go on the streetcorners and set his Cap by his feet. Or for love, like when Babette comes to sit with me and tell gossip things to make the Time pass if I'm blue or the Arthuritis is giving me connimptions or I've got too much Tea into me. I'm bad Company then and I know it, but she comes anyway, bless her, and we fight over nothing till I feel better.*

*Mister Fleur used to say to our Talent: "Look, Boys and Girls, it's not just Fun they want. They like to make it seem so because they know the rest lies too deep. What they need is to feel they're Somebody and that Somebody Else notices it. And they want to be touched, so the World*

139

won't chill down to a cold Hurt and the Wind blow through 'em," he'd say. "And don't despise them neither for coming here," he'd say, "because that'd be despising yourselves for being here, and I won't have that. Anybody works here is good enough for me, and that means good enough for the fucking World."

Maybe they could nail a man for talking so nowadays, the way the Righteousness is thickening up in Nuber like milk going sour in the jug. We're protecting Democracy and Liberty these days, and that means you better walk soft and not bother the Brass.

We got a new Musician, for my Money he ain't worth a Dam. Takes his pay mainly in meals and Trade, that's all right. Has a Gitter and does some songs pretty good, Old-Time Rock he calls them, he forgets I was a grown-up already when the original was still in Style, me and Sam and Stevie oftentimes laying around making love to it when we didn't feel like hearing real music. This is a Nice-Enough Boy, but for a Professor you don't want a Boy, you want a man that's had Trouble and Joy so's to give him what I guess the Abramites call a Soul-Ripening. Babette she picked him up to ripen, someplace.

I call him Joe which is his Name. The Girls can call him Professor if they want, not me. Taking it in Trade, he favors Glorie mostly, she being stacked the biggest. Yesterday morning I heard a Commotion in the Room where Demetrios and Solitaire and the Professor used to be, and there they was, him and Glorie, helling around bare-ass. I could see they'd been prying into things. I know we got to use that room for Business, but Babette hadn't finished doing it out. That bitch Glorie had spread out some of Solitaire's things that had to be left behind—to steal and sell likely—half her ass would be enough to split Solitaire's things. I chased them out with a Scolding, because it did give me a turn to see them grunting and frenching all over Demetrios's Bed.

Some of our Regulars are already saying, "Where's Demetrios, what about the Stories we used to have into the Parlor?" All Joe knows is a few flat old porn tales everybody heard before the year umph.

140

*I started to say, I think Entertainment means building a Special Place, call it a Special World, where other people can come and forget the bloody one they got to live in Most of the Time. Like Mister Fleur made this place, and didn't little Shawn make a World too with his crazy Pictures? And my old Demetrios. Or maybe I'm talking about something bigger than Entertainment, if there is anything bigger. No, I don't believe there could be any grander Occupation than making Worlds, especially if other people can come into them, like I would have made a World for Marcus if I could.*

In the morning the Company explored Trottersville, to kill time before the Circus. T.S. had given free passes for them all, and would have been hurt by a suggestion that he'd never get rich that way.

Nobody gets rich in Trottersville except the Patrons, the landowning families, and they've already got it. Some artisans and businessmen like the innkeeper, who call themselves Burjoyces, manage to stay comfortable. The Guilt Craftsmen run small shops, but all essential stores are owned by the Patrons: Welfare People trade there or do without. Angus, nosing around to learn things, was told the Welfare People are so named because Society has their Welfare at heart. They rent small strips of land for subsistence, in return for spending two-thirds of their labor time on the Patrons' fields. It is a Free Democracy: in their free hours they may do as they please so long as they stay home. The penalty for a first attempt to leave the district is the loss of one ear. The second attempt is usually the last.

Trottersville is in touch by fairly good roads with a nation in the south called Virginia, importing ideas as well as the tea, silk, and cotton we like so much, even though it's produced by that slave labor which is totally unheard-of in the Free Democracies. The manager of the Trottersville Importers' Guilt told Angus that the Welfare System had been working fine all through the Christian Era, and did he think he could figure out a better one? Also, if he wanted to criticize, him and his dog could gosemplace someplace else to do it.

141

Angus wasn't criticizing, he just wanted to find out. More and more, he said to Demetrios that day, he was wanting to find out things. An old hunger never satisfied in the Inner City at Nuber (except by the books!). "The people I knew couldn't imagine I really wanted truth, if truth was any-way uncomfortable or unfashionable." He sat over drinks with Demetrios at the tavern; the others were still out savoring the town and would meet them at the circus lot. "But I did want to find out things, Demetrios, and I do. To find out why for instance that old war ever happened forty-seven years ago. And how different was it essentially from the war that's bound to happen between Moha and Katskil in the next few years because both silly little nations want to exploit the old mines near the borders?"

"Weaponry is the main difference, perhaps. We can't destroy life on the grand scale any more, unless some new technology is built up, and there may not be the resources for that. The difference in weaponry makes a psychological difference. There'll be small medieval wars, with man-to-man confrontation, the warrior's dearest thrill—you remember your Iliad?—and no button-pushing. But it's still war, and we'll have it because we're too stupid to read history, and not brave or intelligent enough to respect our fellow beings."

"Respect, not love. Thou art bitter, Demetrios." Demetrios was not feeling bitter. He was suffering, but pleasantly, from the beauty of Angus's hands, the gentleness of his mouth, a waterfall of light across his shoulder. "Thee and thou—we spoke that way now and then at Inner City. A sometime thing with me—you can even use it along with the modern way."

"I like it, Angus. In Outer City it was usually sneered at . . . Yes, respect. Love is for individuals. Whoever claims to love humanity is a hypocrite or self-deceiver. We love men and women and children, not abstractions. But the concept Man is worthy of respect, and in a climate of respect something politically decent might some day emerge. The American states made a beginning at the end of the 18th Century, but couldn't protect the achievement from watergating and other corruption . . . Nobody loves

142

Man, poor monster. An artist doesn't love his art, either —he lives within it and for it, is carried by it, but love has no meaning in that connection that I can see. I love, thou lovest—love is for thee and Solitaire—tell me, is it good between you?"

"Very good, man Demetrios."

"It's for Garth and Frankie, for Solitaire and me. For thee and me, Angus." He covered the boy's hands; they responded.

"Is there the body's need in it?"

"I'm old, and yet I don't think I'd care to die without having embraced thee."

"The serpent in Eden—wasn't its name Jealousy?"

"My God!" said Demetrios—"you've given me another story."

Angus grinned. Sobering, he said: "You told me once —it was at the Meadows, the day we met—that love is a country. I like that saying." In Angus there would always be an observer, even a judge, but this took nothing from his warmth—rather, Demetrios thought, it was what made his acceptance a beatitude. "A wide country," said Angus, "with many roads, and no place to walk timidly. I'll always need you, now and long after you're dead, my friend."

Sawyer Finn's circus possessed no tent, and so had made Smallways' back forty like a fairground. An area had been roped off where a slope of land allowed a low semicircular theater. The public could settle there or stroll among the exhibition tents, after paying admission at the gate of Smallways' fence, where Frankie and Solitaire were watching for Demetrios and Angus; the others had gone in with their free passes. "H.F. says it'll be a real bully circus."

"But he's worried, Frankie?" Demetrios asked.

Solitaire kissed Angus and rolled her forehead on his chest. "Little cat," he murmured.

"Little pregnant cat. Demetrios's fruit'll be a man-child."

"They're worried," said Frankie, his underlip stuck out in bother. "Mr. Virgil says the yucks are coming in too quiet."

"I'm Mr. Virgil," said the man with the handlebar mustaches, who was attending the gate. No more folk were

143

arriving; the crowd already inside was small. "I have the puma act, and it's account of them we can't let the dog in—I'm really sorry, he's a beauty. Frankie has known me a long time—twenty minutes—so he figured you did."

"Up yours too," said Frankie gently, preoccupied.

"I'll stay out here with Brand a while," Angus said. "Then someone else can take my place with him and I'll go in. But he never pulls when I have him leashed."

"It's the smell. It would make the cats act up."

"Sure."

"Nice if everybody was obliging like you," said Mr. Virgil. "It's a fact, they been coming in too quiet, like people do when they might be looking for trouble."

"Don't see many kids," said Demetrios.

"Ain't many in Trottersville. It's that kind of town."

Frankie said: "Can't people just enjoy themselves and be nice instead of all the time trouble-trouble? Especially at a *Circus?*" With Demetrios he returned to the circus ground, but at a black tent marked with cabalistic signs he said: "Oh, that's just old Blynken—" and ran off about his own researches.

Demetrios ducked his head to enter candle-lit darkness, where little Blynken sat alone at a table with two chairs, peering into a crystal ball. "Draw thou the Inner Curtain, that none may—oh, it's you, hi! Draw it anyway. It's got a 'busy' sign—pity most of the yucks can't read." She lifted off a spangled turban. "T.S. had this damn contraption made years ago for somebody with too much skull. I heard a rustling in it up there a while ago, like mice." She tidied her fine red hair. "Sit. Is it filling up any out there?"

"Not much. Mr. Virgil doesn't like the look of it."

"Ayah, and he's got experience! Hold my hand, dear —if anyone busts in I'm reading your palm. Or shall I, for real? Living does write on us, though not the way they think. What a nice old gardener's fist! . . . Wynken was crying most of the night."

"Oh?"

"Bundle of nerves, and today she and Nod must dance on horseback. She wants us to go with your Company,

144

Demetrios, if you'll have us. So do I, so does Nod I think, only he hates quick decisions."

"It would be a joy to us. But we hardly know where we're going, Blynken. 'West' is only a word, and the world's round."

"Don't you really, my dear? . . . Well, for us, the way things happen, Sawyer Finn's Circus took us in at a time when we needed them but they didn't truly need us. It was the old boys' kindness. Mr. Virgil's wife is better at the fortune-telling pitch than I am, but I had to fit in somewhere. Now she takes care of the commissary, laundry and all-what-all—claims she prefers it. I feel temporary. T.S. and H.F.—God, sometimes you'd almost think they *were*—" she studied him, perhaps testing his acceptance and compassion.

"It would be a delight, any time," said Demetrios, "to talk with you about the different facets of truth. We'd never run short."

"And I could serve tea. Well, T.S. talks about retiring, but it would break his heart. H.F. says more sensibly: 'Looky, Tom, I been retired all my life and what good did it ever do me?' But we're a different sort of freaks, modern freaks at that. New-century people."

"Like T.S. and H.F. I live in both worlds, at home in neither."

"Where's home, ever? We're not at home here, we three, but—oh, it's hard even to think about a break!"

"Was that the only reason Wynken was crying?"

"No, sweet man." Blynken looked away, head tilted, listening to crowd sounds beyond the tent. "God, I wish I was small enough to be in their act! No, she was thinking of Frankie, and of all young people the way they are before the world rolls over them."

"Nothing new-century about that, Blynken."

"For sure, for true! It's our covenant with nature—Wynken said that, last night: so much to enjoy if we can, and then return the raw materials. But—so short a time for being Frankie!"

"That other almost-question you almost asked: no, I really couldn't tell you where our Company is going. But I think, as an old man may, of a republic growing up, slowly, isolated for a while in a rather empty world with a number of slag heaps—growing up from a beginning made by this handful of human beings who are traveling with me. I didn't choose them—that man Bosco will probably leave us to look for a certain Rambler gang—"

"I hope he does. I didn't like him."

"Oh—probably no real harm in him."

"There is," said Blynken—"no, never mind, I may be wrong. Go on, tell me more, Demetrios."

"Well, I didn't choose them and I don't lead them— but the potential of generous leadership is there against the time it's needed. Love and chance drew us together, and I begin to see we have certain qualities in common, qualities that were never of much influence in Old Time: we are able, for instance, to love without jealousy. We can enjoy remaining separate beings while we cherish the community that we have with each other."

"Was jealousy so great a thing in Old Time?"

"I was thirteen, the year of the Crash. I saw little jealousy, but mine was a rare sort of family for the 1990s —they gave me education as well as love. The social tradition was loaded with jealousy, and there were still people who made a virtue of it. That had begun to change twenty or thirty years before I was born. Some of the young people of the 1960s and '70s were able to bring peace and generosity into the sexual freedom that earlier generations had won only part-way and in bitterness. The Crash put an end to many bright promises. Well, our Company has faults, and we haven't been much tested yet, but so far I've seen no cruelty or meanness, no grabbing, no greed."

"There's been none with us three, Demetrios. Nod and Wynken and I have been natural lovers for more than three years."

"I think it can happen only for small groups, small enough to keep sensitive person-to-person communication —that's the heart of it. Old Time at its worst was an urban thing, unable to comprehend the importance of small groups. The mass communications that should have been a simple public service became a dominating horror of homogenized stupidity. The small groups themselves forgot their importance, yielded up the virtue of town meeting without a struggle. You'd think they could have remembered that the family or tribe or commune family is the servant of the individual. It's Frankenstein's original necessary monster, and must not be permitted to turn on its maker, or hell is loose. The village, a larger monster, is the servant of the family, and the far-off central government, if there must be one, greatest and ugliest monster of all, is still by rights the servant of the village, and ought to be in direct communication with it, directly answerable. But in the uproars and terrors of Old Time, this simple idea, the obvious essence of representative government, could scarcely even make itself heard. Impractical! Impractical! And of course it was, once the swollen political and corporate growths had become inoperable. . . . Well, maybe what our Company starts with won't carry through. Making a republic is a labor for the gods, and we aren't gods. But I have this old man's thought, and I have my hopeful moments."

"We need an island," said Blynken. "An island meeting certain specifications."

Demetrios was happy. Often later he would enjoy this ability Blynken had to take what you say as a creation to be shared, as if with your four hands you held up a new picture and considered, artists with a common devotion, what more might be done to make it live.

The crowd noise changed. "Hell, that's trouble!" said Blynken; she jumped up to fling open the curtain. "Stay with me, friend, and hang onto that stick."

Sunshine hit their eyes. People were running in it—not many, but they were high with that tension, that witless gap-mouthed hunger for a spectacle of disaster, which can make a few look and smell like a multitude. They were running and stumbling down toward the stage area, the level ground below the natural theater, and down there, like flowers tossed about in a water-bucket, gaudily dressed Wynken and Nod were trying to keep their footing on the bare backs of their horses. Yesterday the beasts had been gentle snufflers; Demetrios had petted them, and seen Wynken and Frankie and Nod climb around all over them. Now they had gone mad.

They reared and plunged, Wynken's beast choking,

147

Nod's venting a wild, miserable scream. H.F. managed to grab the bridle Wynken had lost, and was thrown about like an old stick. Garth running to help him shouted to Demetrios: "The bastards spooked them—clods, with pepper! They think it's funny."

As Demetrios hurried down—Blynken had already darted far ahead of him—he saw Wynken lose her balance and tumble asprawl of the horse's tossing, writhing neck, saving herself with a clutch of his mane; and the crowd yelled with delight. One voice squawked out above the rest: "Make with the porn show, Baby! Strip!" Others took it up, finding a rhythm: "Strip! Strip! Baby, strip!"

Nod vaulted down. He wrenched his horse's head around, and with a slap and a yell sent the beast running blind toward the spectators, whose laughter ceased. Somewhere among them Bosco had just picked up somebody and thrown him at somebody else.

By the watch on Angus's wrist, the Battle of Trottersville began at 3:01 P.M., Friday, July 26, 47, when he heard trouble and pushed through the gate with Brand a leashed storm at the end of his arm, reached a climactic point when a crow-voiced yuck hollered: "Let's clean up the joint!" and a higher point when Angus hit him. It ended at 3:05 when Frankie jumped on a barrel and yelled: "Run for your lives! The pumas is loose!"

T.S. later told Frankie that this was the noblest lie of the Year 47—no, more likely the noblest of the decade, or say the century. It had cost Frankie almost sixty seconds to arrange it with Mr. Virgil and help him wheel the cage out of sight behind a caravan and cover it with a tarp.

During the four minutes Demetrios's stick had connected with at least one skull—he hoped it belonged to the one who had yelled for a porn show, but there was too much dust to be sure. He witnessed Angus's arrival with Brand, and rested a bit, panting but able to relish it when Brand tore off somebody's loin-rag before Angus saw fit to restrain him. The man had looked almost like a policeman before he lost his modesty and ran for it, but that could hardly be—likely Demetrios's fevered imagination. On the whole, a lovely fight, though too much exertion for one of his years.

There were other head-smashings and arguments. Wynken had been able to jump down clear when Garth quieted her horse; H.F. scooped her up and ran with her on his shaky legs to the shelter of a caravan. After that Demetrios had the soothing impression of Garth and Angus hitting a lot of people, with aid and advice from T.S.

But Frankie decided the day. After his shot it was all over. The beat and the elite of Trottersville retired from the field like piss off the end of a dock.

# CHAPTER THIRTEEN

*Nothing is just too big, you can't look at it.*

> *And I turned myself to behold wisdom, and madness,*
> *and folly: for what can the man do that cometh after*
> *the king? even that which hath been already done.*
> *Then I saw that wisdom excelleth folly, as far as*
> *light excelleth darkness.*
> *—ECCLESIASTES, II: 12, 13.*

The Company and Sawyer Finn's Circus considered it
intelligent, after decent reflection, to split, and the Company gladly accepted the offer of a ride as far as the next
crossroad that led north.

The farm of Jason Smallways lay to the west of Trottersville. Angus, Brand, and Bosco made a portentous progress
back there to pick up the gear still at the tavern. Angus
showed a black eye and Brand two red ones; Bosco was
moved to roll his muscles like a bear; nobody bothered
them. None of their stuff had been stolen except one ham,
and Bosco said never mind, there might be some way to
correct this. On their safe return, the rest of the day was
spent in nursing bruises and readying for a departure at
dawn.

Night travel is unsafe anywhere but especially in Penn,
where the most convincing tales of brown tiger come
from. He has (folk say) attacked villages down there and
carried off people, sometimes haunting a particular region
for weeks or months like a burning conscience. Tawny
stripes, they say, on a pelt like a cloud of white and cin-
namon. The stripes melt into the colors of morning or
evening, and if you see him at all at those hours it's probably too late.

150

T.S. wanted to go north. He had a hankering to take the Circus all the way to Nova Scotia where the evangelines are, and though Demetrios warned him they might not be there now—it's the change of climate, evangelines need the northern winters or something—still T.S. allowed he'd give it a whirl. But the Company wanted west—two moonshines are as good as daylight, maybe. And it was that night, in the good quiet, with the drinks, the music, the campfire mood, that we agreed Wynken, Blynken, and Nod would go with the Company.

Never forgetting Brand, the Company was eleven.

That settled, T.S. kissed all the girls including Solitaire goodnight and pottered off to bed. H.F. sat up a while to hear Demetrios tell the story of how brown tiger might have come to haunt this part of the world where no such beast was ever known in the past. It's a story of one of those mad saints who bloomed in such profusion in the dying years of Old Time. Not long before the war, this fellow slunk about to the zoos in several of the great cities, liberating the beasts under cover of night, burning off locks with what was called a blowtorch. Some believed he was not one man but a group of conspirators. One man, Demetrios thought. Anyhow the episodes ended after that one man, who kept a diary and called himself Jack the Liberator, was found gored to death by a Cape buffalo he had let loose. It's a harsh, sad little tale—Jack had no love for the animals, he just hated the world—and your novelist may write it some day remembering Demetrios's words, but not here. Among the creatures set free by Jack was a pair of Manchurian tigers, the female already heavy with young.

H.F. went to bed too, not forgetting to kiss the girls. Bosco had slipped off somewhere, his absence for a long time unnoticed. All were comfortable and lazy, but even Frankie not yet sleepy (our hero) so in this hour the new members saw fit to tell their new friends something of what the world had done to them and they to the world, since they would now be sharing joy and trouble and love and danger with Demetrios's people all the way to the other ocean.

"Nod," said Wynken, "was born Seiji Ohara, the last

151

name being a good Irish one even without the apostrophe, as had been noted by his great-grandfather Seumas O'Hara when he arrived in Boston from Bally na Hinch in 1854, not very skilled in the English spelling of foreign names—that is, when the apostrophe dropped he was not after stooping to pick it up. Thus it came about—"

"—that we skip a generation," said Blynken, "arriving at the marriage of his grandson Stockton Ohara late in life to Teru Kamayatsu who in 1985 turned up in that course on *The Socio-Ideological Matrix of Piers Plowman* which Stockton was then conducting at a well-thought-of university located in Cambridge, Massachusetts. For some years they were childless. Stockton in his sixties, having undergone an unusual number of diagnostic X rays in addition to the atmospheric and other radioactive pollution which was politely referred to as normal, believed himself to be sterile. In 1992 he retired from teaching, and the two went to live in the town of Hoton near the New Hampshire border, where they were when the war came. Though untouched by bombing effects apart from radiation, the town was severely damaged by the earthquakes of the Year One, and decimated by the plagues. It was hardly more than a camp site in the ruins when, in the Year Four, there was born unexpectedly to Teru and Stockton Ohara a son—"

"—who is now forty-three," said Nod, "and looks it, being thus two years older than his beloved though garrulous wives. They were born, Wynken being the older by two hours, at another small but famous town in Massachusetts, in the Year Six. Their father Ignace Kabotski, who had been a child refugee from Poland in the European famine of 1978 and who never—"

Solitaire cried: "But Wynken *can't* be over twenty-five!"

"Love, I'm forty-one," Wynken said, not looking at Frankie.

"But with my crow's feet and double chin I show it," said Blynken.

"You imagine them," said Wynken. "On me of course *every* old thing is so small it doesn't show."

"Anyhow what looks like my middle-aged sag is actually—"

"O beautiful!" said Solitaire. "This too."

"Maybe we can pop together," said Blynken.

"If I may now again intrude, their father Ignace Kabotski, a refugee who never did change his name to Cabot in spite of Blynken's tendency to say he did, really a deplorable inverted snobbery—"

"A natural defense," said Wynken. "Even after the war the town was full of stuffpots. We grew up with 'em."

"Ignace Kabotski," said Nod, "was the acknowledged leader in the effort to hold that town together after the Crash, stuffpots and all. The mother of the girls died in an outbreak of diphtheria in the Year Nine, so they but dimly remember her. By the time the twins (obviously not identical) were out of early childhood, it was evident that Wynken would be, as I am, what people call a midget, while Blynken would grow to normal or almost normal size. Ignace believed in the virtues of learning, a conviction strengthened by the calamities of his century. He held that there are only two important ways to avoid the consequences of folly: one, to act with wisdom; two, never to get born. Since wisdom is an acquired quality, he set himself with devotion to give his daughters the firmest and widest education he could manage under the difficulties, a training which—"

"—even now renders us capable," said Wynken, "of sharing the bewilderment of this boy Seiji Ohara growing up in surroundings where an accepted and tolerated desolation was the norm. Hoton was a ruin inhabited by slow-moving giants with broken hearts. Compassion usually comes late in adolescence if one is to learn it at all. That was so with Seiji, intensely impatient with these big dazed people while they were all he knew, full of pity later when they'd been swept off the earth. He loved his mother, but she too was existing in a state of shock, almost as hazy as the rest of them. Seiji's old father—accustomed to teaching the fantastics of medievalism, and to grown-ups—did his best to supply what basic education he could: reading, writing, figuring, enough history for a start. He died when Seiji was twelve. Teru carried on as best she could—Seiji was not a manageable brat. She still believed when he was fourteen that he might have a spurt of growth, though his hands and feet never had the puppy largeness of a growing boy's. The loneliness of Hoton was extreme, partly—"

"—because of ancient vanities," said Blynken. "After the war most stricken groups wanted to join others, as you've told us wanderers drifted into Nuber. Not so in Hoton, nor in Lowelltown. They still felt the world ought to come to them; when it did, it might come with witless cruelty. Sitting still, waiting for better times, those ghost towns were easy prey for outlaws, wild folk, the new savages. In his fifteenth year Seiji was working with his mother in their corn patch when three horsemen came storming out of nowhere and snatched up Teru. Seiji they flung aside—"

"I bit the wrist of the one that caught me up and felt it crunch. He yelled, I landed in the dirt, and they were gone."

"Then he saw others of the band setting fires and butchering his neighbors for pleasure. He escaped into the woods, and was joined by a few survivors from Hoton and other ravaged towns. They formed their own wild crew. They valued Seiji in spite of his smallness because for a while he was fiercer than any giant, and quicker than the rest of them to learn woodcraft and hunting. His speed and silence in the wilderness are uncanny. He took part in certain acts of reprisal—"

"—which he prefers not to remember," said Nod. "We never caught up with the men who took my mother. When I was seventeen I understood we were simply turning into bandits ourselves, no better than the rest. I left them, lived in the wilderness alone for two years, visiting human habitations as a listening shadow. I needed little. Arrowheads I flaked out from the flint, still do. Worth the effort —with my light bow I prefer them. When in need of something that couldn't be had except by stealing, it was—"

"—his whim to leave something in exchange," said Wynken, "such as a rabbit pelt for a hank of yarn."

Mr. Virgil remarked: "Woe unto anyone else who talked in so."

"They don't know the signals, man Virgil," said Wynken.

"They didn't murder me," said Solitaire.

"Well, you're a sweet kid," said Nod. "We make exceptions."

"Actually more than a whim," Wynken continued, "for Seiji was then and is now more ethically decent than his wretched little wives, who seek to profit by his example yet make at times but a halting progress, hm. (You used the first person singular, Solitaire honey.) They had, it's true, that education he mentioned, but it sometimes abandons them. It had, when Seiji first observed them out of his forest invisibility, as they stumbled down an empty road without any idea where they were going, because the wits had been knocked clean out of them. At that time they could have been called temporary idiots. You see, Lowelltown also was wiped out, by sickness. We don't even know what the epidemic was. There weren't any Old-Time doctors left there; it may have been a new thing anyway—violent fever, rash, glandular swellings, sudden collapse. The town had survived the postwar plagues, diphtheria, the red plague of Year Sixteen, but this one cleared the slate. I mean—*everyone*, except my sister and me, the beauty and the midget, explain it how you will. When we grasped what had happened we only thought of getting out, going down the road, no goal except escape. Blynken, whom I knew then as Sophia, wanted—"

"—to die, or so I said, but you made me lie down in the shade, Miranda, and took my head in your lap and said to me: 'No, you will live—' and so I lived. For a while I slept so deeply that one world fell away from me, though—"

"—all the worlds," said Nod, "may be full of illusion as well as truth, and their philosophers amazed."

"And when she woke Nod had already come to us, standing there naked and beautiful, with his bow—"

"—and hardly taller than you, Miranda. So my thoughts went racing down the millennia, every one of them a praise of life—"

"—and the wind had played with the hair on your forehead while you slept, your breasts were white and virgin."

"And the first words he spoke after Blynken's waking were: 'Come with me so we can care for each other and not be lonely.' "

"Therefore I knew he was of finer substance than the gods, namely flesh and blood. And now I will explain our names, but I'll do it in a subdued tone of voice because our hero, without whom Sawyer Finn's Circus might well be lying in ruins, appears to have fallen asleep. The explanation is simple: our mother whom we don't quite remember knew that funny old poem and a bit of music for it, and sang us to sleep with it, and so did our father after she died, and—"

"—sometimes you sang it for me when I was drowsy in the hot afternoons or the nights in the forest and the other places we've known, so that I learned it. And I sang it for you, Wynken, when sleep abandoned you in the bad time after our baby was lost. Then when we happened on the Circus, and T.S. so kindly invited us to join them, and asked our names, we thought, why not name ourselves after a fragment of Old-Time fancy? Though it's true that we are spirits of another sort, still, Shakespeare is not for all occasions, and—ayah," said Nod, "Frankie's asleep for sure. Sounds like a very small porpoise."

"Where did you ever—"

"—hear a very small porpoise?"

"In your dreams."

[*Saturday, August 24*]

*It's more than a month my old Demetrios has been gone, and sometimes Babette and me play wonder-what about what's happened to them. But that Game can't feed on Nothing. Babette said today, Nothing is just too big, you can't look at it.*

*Professor was the First. Seems to me it was twelve years ago he turned up on my back Porch with his Lute, and played, and looked at me in his Particular Way. And was it ten years ago Demetrios came to me?—I get mixed. Before Babette anyhow. Solitaire was here only two years, but I did Love her more than any of them knew. Not wanting to get in bed with her like I've done with Fran sometimes, not Motherly neither but still a wanting-to-help Love, for it was strongest in the Times when she got wild, it was like seeing an Angel in a Spiderweb.*

*Me and Babette pretty well know, though we don't say*

156

*it, that we ain't likely to see those three again, nor Garth
and his cockahoop little Brother, nor that young Ristacrat
—he was all right, I liked him. I think he'll do Solitaire
good, anyway he'll try. And that Character Dimmy picked
up in the Jail, Babette said he was the Practical Type.
Well, but if they do come back it won't be soon, and
there's that lump in my right breast.*

*I hope I don't go talking to Babette about that just for
lonesomeness, because what could she do? There ain't an
Old-Time Doctor in all Nuber, and any new-time Surgeon
likely makes his living as a Barber, they can Keep That.
I believe I can wait my time without too much fuss, I
wouldn't be the First and won't be the Last. Why would
anybody be afraid of Death unless he'd talked himself into
thinking there's an afterlife? I couldn't do that. I tried,
after Marcus, was still trying when I came to Nuber,
though Myself kept saying to me inside, You Fool, it ain't
wishing anything will make it so.*

*Mr. Fleur he knew how it was with me. He said to me,
quiet and kind, he says, "Stell, you ever black out?" I said
yes I had, couple times. He says: "It has to be like that.
No blood moving in the Brain nor breath in the Lungs,
why, no Thinking, no Feeling. No Thinking and Feeling
no Person. Don't despise the Body, Stell," he says. "No
Body, no Mind." I've been quiet inside about it, since.*

*Dying, yes, we can be excused for hating that, that seems
like a bad Animal coming after you. But more than half of
that is just Funk, like being afraid of the Dark. I guess
when the Tiger picks you up, you anyhow know it won't
be long.*

*Lately I've took to the habit of carrying a Stick to lean
on when I go out into my Garden, I know why it was
Demetrios liked to have one, only for me it's the Arthuritis
made me think of it. Suppose I write about Something I
seen in the Garden a while ago, when I was Poking around.*

*That fella Joe is doing a mite better on the Janitor Work,
but he don't so far give the Garden no more than a Licking and a Promise. Babette she keeps after him, tries. He
can always find new ways of resting onto the job. Some
places that my old Demetrios kept neatened up has already
gone to weeds in the time he's been gone. I tell Babette,*

*Don't sweat Joe too much, he's got to ease into it like Gradual, and maybe weeding does bother his Gitter Fingers. Maybe it do, she says, only Professor never minded pulling weeds, he'd do it for love, not ast. Joe ain't Professor, I said to her, so let him grow up a little. Anyhow—*

*There's this stretch in the Border where Demetrios has set out Lilies for me, time to time, some the neighbors have give me and some he's found around the Countryside where Old-Time people used to have Gardens. There's early-blooming white ones, and some big fragrant Whites with a goldy center, Regals Demetrios called them, and a fawny tan one, and of course the common kinds too, some being Day-Lilies and Tiger Lilies like I remember growing wild in Raeburn. So I was out there in the deep Sunlight leaning onto my cane, and thinking back I suppose—that's natural. Then I seen how the grass and wild convolvulus and Things had gone to growing thick where Joe hadn't done nothing. So I felt bad about that, I even started for to reach and pull, but the Arthuritis knocked that idear out of me, fast. But further down the Border I come on a gaudy common Tiger Lily standing in the sun with his sword-leaves and funny black knobs and his buds opening out full. There was this convolvulus wropping itself around him, and a Catmint crowding him along with the rank Grass. He just stood there looking like my old Demetrios. He didn't mind, he made me think of any good man or woman in the sun, with a burden but carrying it, and with Time left over to recognize me. That was all—I felt better and went back in the House and had my Tea.*

*It's only the having to stop that gripes us. Having to stop even the small things, the good Breakfast or a touch of the Corn Spirit, or Music heard someplace down the Street, or seeing a new Face with something sweet in it, or an old face with something New.*

*But we stop.*

Garth and the other grown-ups sat up a while worrying about Bosco, which was unnecessary at least so far as the man's physical safety was concerned. H.F.—not sleeping well these days, he said—emerged in nightshirt and slippers to help them worry. He had been sorry not to be able to

158

tell Bosco anything useful about Gammo's Ramblers. Some three or four years ago the Circus had entered a town up in northern Moha which had only just donated all its loose change to a Rambler company of that name, and T.S. had taken pains to learn what way the Ramblers had gone, so as not to meet them again under those conditions. Gammo's Ramblers were heading west, but that was all he knew; Bosco had taken it philosophically.

Bosco returned at about midnight, soft-footed, with a ham under his arm and a chicken carcass dangling. "Could even be the same ham," he said proudly. Seeing Demetrios's distress, Angus's disapproval, Garth's startled anxiety, Bosco grew sulky. "Well, I figured the chicken's a sort of commission—you know?"

"Seeing what they done about your ham," said H.F. uncomfortably, "I reckon you could say tit for tat, still it don't seem just right, Bosco. T.S. ain't going to like it. T.S. is going to call it stealing, a body shouldn't do it. Did you have to bust into a house?"

"Woodshed," said Bosco meekly enough, perhaps respecting something venerable in Demetrios as well as in H.F. But the meekness itself was not pleasant. For some time Demetrios had been finding it difficult to adjust his republic to the presence of Bosco as a citizen—but then, where was the republic? "Jasus!" said Bosco—"I figured you'd be pleased." Nobody said anything. Bosco searched Garth's face with especial intentness, and got no comfort from it. "Well, Jasus, you going to be down on me just for picking up something, maybe I better skin out. I won't stick around where I ain't wanted. I can just take my ham and my goddamn chicken and by God split."

"No need of that," said Demetrios, and wondered if he meant that at all. Leadership was not in him.

"So long as you know," said Angus, "how the Company feels about it, stay with us, Bosco. Stay and learn our ways." No one of them before, so far as Demetrios remembered, had spoken of the Company in just that way, with that authority. He could not have done it himself without self-consciousness.

"Well, Jasus—" Bosco was unlikely to learn much, but

159

Angus might have said the most assuring thing as well as the right one.

"We done things thataway," said Garth, "we'd be in hot water all the time, Bosco. We got to treat people by rules they understand, right? Like if a bunch of 'em come after you now for busting into that shed, everybody'd get hurt, and maybe we couldn't turn them pumas loose a second time."

That seemed to reach Bosco. He rumbled miserably, flung down the ham and chicken, brushed his hands. "Well, Jasus—"

"I figure," said H.F., yawning, "you was tempted beyond your stren'th, Bosco. It's a noble ham."

Bosco allowed his feathers to be smoothed; the Company went to bed in peace. We lent a hand getting the circus wagons under way at dawn (Bosco working harder than anyone) and rode along in them all through the morning.

At about the noon hour we halted by a crossroad for a meal with ham in it. Then, after many loving farewells, after T.S. had scrupulously paid their back wages to Wynken, Blynken, and Nod, and got a receipt for it, after T.S. and H.F. had kissed all the girls (Blynken blubbering a little bit), Sawyer Finn's Circus took the northern road, and though the road leading west dimmed out in grass, we found others after a while. It is not hard to travel by the sun. When the sun goes down in glory it's time to sleep; when it rises all you need do is hold it behind you till the noon, and rest, and go on to the end of the day.

*As your novelist, I too regret that you should be some-what losing awareness of Demetrios's viewpoint. But viewpoints (what an odd, inaccurate word!)—viewpoints do fade, even cease. It engages my vanity that I have been able to give you as much of his as I have—but there, I knew the man well, as they say, and spent many hours in talk with him, rambling, observing, questioning in my sly manner, so that if there's anything in his life, even from the faraway beginnings in Hesterville and including the details of the years in Nuber, the fun and troubles of the sex-house, the garden he tended, the worries over Mam Estelle and her tea or the sound of Elizabeth of Hartford*

160

*beating up a cookie batter with an Old-Time spoon and
bowl—if there's any of that I don't either know or have
snugged down in my notebooks, it's hardly worth mentioning. The notebooks made up a good deal of the weight
in my bac-pac till I talked Garth into carrying some of
them for me. I believe I told you Garth couldn't read.
Angus and Demetrios fixed that, and he was a quick study,
not a passionate spark like Frankie but bright and eager
for discoveries, but my tiny marks in the notebooks are a
shorthand of my own. Besides, Garth was always a sweet
kid, and wouldn't have peeked without permission. I could
use his viewpoint (some time I intend to analyze that
word; not as absurd as "standpoint" but still pretty crazy)
—his viewpoint too if I was amind to: an adolescent boy is
not really any more fantastic than other warm-blooded
animals.*

Demetrios's viewpoint (the reader may now supply his
own exegesis, since the novelist is out of sight again)
was becoming somewhat clouded by forgetfulness, that
mental cataract. There was also the worm of pain that
more often made its journey up and down in his belly and
probed more detestably, and the presence of this creature
was bound to color his thoughts.

A morning came when the rain fell lightly. It would
not have interfered with the Company's traveling, but
Angus decided that they should rest that day, and so they
stayed in the shelter of a fine stone barn that stood sound
where no house was. Rain ceased and the sun appeared
in early afternoon, but Angus said it was too late to start,
also he thought Brand was slightly lame from the chase of
yesterday when Bosco had failed to bring down a deer
with the first arrow. Bosco had been using a new bow
Garth had made for him—Garth handy at anything, and
Frankie ever-present with the sacred Hatchet—and had
been in too much haste for good shooting. "So let's loaf
the rest of the day and chew venison," said Angus. "The
western ocean will wait for us."

It never occurred to Demetrios that the rest was being
called on his account, nor did he notice that when they
continued the following day, travel was slow, with numerous halts.

He enjoyed the new pace, enjoyed the heft of his walnut stick, enjoyed resting in the sun with his back against a tree trunk. Someone was always with him, he noticed—Solitaire, very often Wynken with her small voice and curious green eyes, occasionally Frankie with not much to say, but most often Angus, who was never far off even when someone else was keeping him company.

One day the Professor and Angus were sharing the sunlit shaft of a broad oak with him when he noticed Solitaire in conversation with Blynken, and he saw that Solitaire was disturbed. But it was not one of her trouble-times. In fact, unless his tiresome memory was betraying him (and he had found that it was already interfering with his telling of stories), Solitaire had not gone through any of those storms since the little episode on the approach to Trottersville. And now she merely looked excited, like one who has stumbled on something pleasant—a coin shining in the road, a friend's face in a crowd of strangers—and Demetrios heard her say: "Oh yes, Blynken, do let's pop together, and you can name your baby after mine, and I'll name mine after yours, but Blynken, love, don't ever call me Solitaire! Who was she, this Solitaire? There was never any such person, only me, and I am I, I am I, and my name is Eve."

# CHAPTER FOURTEEN

## When I'm Building I'm Right with Myself

> But we are spirits of another sort.
> —Shakespeare,
> *A MIDSUMMER NIGHT'S DREAM.*

We came by this slow travel into a region where the air held an odor of salt and seaweed, as it sometimes does at Nuber or in the eastern nations when the wind blows from the Atlantic, the ocean that no one crosses in our lifetime, perhaps for many lifetimes to come; but here in the place where Penn has no border, where the known and the wilderness come together with no more sign of joining than there is in the coming together of the sea waves, the wind was blowing out of the southwest, and it was warm. "Salt marsh maybe," said Bosco. "But I can tell you it's durn-much like the air I smelled near the coast of the Freshwater Sea that ain't fresh, that earthquake country of western Moha. I'd think I was there if I didn't know we're way to the south of it."

It was the coast of the inland sea; nothing else could be so immense, so overwhelming with the sense of eternity —and yet it was new, an inflowing of risen waters where recently there had been farmland, forest, cities, roads. New, and old—in earlier millennia, Demetrios had told us, a shallow ocean had covered this land for immeasurable centuries. We were already somewhat south and west of Penn, perhaps. Demetrios had said we would not pass through the town of Aberedo. When Nod asked him how he could be sure of that, the old man's answer was doubtful. He said his journey (he must have meant the journey of all of us) led through time as well as space.

"So does the journey of a rock," said Wynken, "as the turning earth carries it, and the earth's orbit moves with the galaxy." Demetrios looked on her with kindness and some amusement. Wynken is not to everyone's taste, but they had become close friends. Demetrios would have carried her when her little legs grew tired, but in these days he had not quite the strength; the others were burdened with their bac-pacs and similar gear.

"Let Brand carry you," said Angus, and sometimes Wynken did, riding his back for short distances, the gray hound walking proudly and laughing with his tongue at the side of his mouth.

But at this coast our walking had come to an end. A town stood here, with no people in it, and the ancient highway that had brought the Company to it ran down into the sea. No people at all. An empty square, most of the houses fallen in and some overgrown with vines, old street signs dangling, a few. Beyond the abandoned square, into a once-paved open area where even now few seeds had been able to exploit the cracks and make them useful— I think it was what Old Time called a parking lot—into that desolate open space the waters came white-tipped and whispering.

In the west the sea met the horizon, though at the southern section of that arc a rise of hazy blue suggested the presence of land. The sun was shining from behind us on that hinted island, for we had come to this place in middle morning. We saw the strong light touching what may have been a cliffside or waterfall, and Demetrios described this for Angus. Then they moved further away, and I saw them standing at the very edge of the small waves, Demetrios still speaking, but too low for me to hear, his left arm over Angus's shoulders, his other hand with the oaken stick pointing here and there—but it was Demetrios whom the boy's nearsighted eyes were watching, with trouble and tenderness; and it's true that island to the south was so far from us you'd think only a dream could reach it.

Now earlier that morning we had passed an old signboard carrying several names, with figures after them indicating distances, and it seems to me that one of the

164

names may have been Aberedo. Yet Demetrios did not speak of it, and he looked on this ruin of a town with no sign of sorrow or recognition, asking Garth—possibly he meant it at first only as one of his mild jokes—whether he knew how to build a boat to go on with.

"No, man Demetrios," says Garth, serious as always, "but you tell me how, and if it's made of wood and I ain't hurried, I believe I can do it."

"September's a-going toward winter," said Bosco. "Couple months, like. Shelter of a house, even one of them wrecks, would be handy, if it takes till cold weather to build your boat."

"What about repairing one house to live in," said Nod, "in case we're still here when it gets chilly, and using the rest for lumber to build our boat?"

He said "our"; Bosco had said "your"; likely the whole Company noted it.

We discussed the idea comfortably through a lunch that was embellished by apples from someone's long-ago garden, where we sat protected from a brisk damp ocean wind. It seemed a good idea: practical, reasonable, and foolish enough to be interesting. "If my baby is born at sea," said Eve who had been Solitaire, "he'll live long and always be safe in a storm. It's an old Lowelltown superstition, right?"

"Tell 'em how old," says Wynken.

"A day old. Blynken made it up for me yesterday while we were cooking bacon and comparing bulges."

"Hours and hours and hours ago," said Blynken. "Mine are bigger than thine."

"Phoo."

"I can't help it," said Nod, "I love all those women. Well, I'm in favor of the boat. We'll need smoked meat. I'll be hunting while Garth is building."

"We want an island. Demetrios and I were getting that settled when Frankie turned the pumas loose."

"And rode the big one three times around the lot," said Frankie. "Don't leave that out."

"That island we see from here," said Demetrios, "is not really far away. Maybe we'll want something further off. If there's to be another republic—another attempt to make a republic—it might need to grow awhile, undisturbed by the efforts of worried strangers to destroy it." He looked at the Professor, who was usually ready to confirm or deny the good sense of his remarks; the Professor nodded. "Let our island be one not too easily discovered," said Demetrios, "and large enough to support a few hundred or a few thousand souls with a taste for love and a taste for privacy."

Thus it was agreed—though Bosco made a production of saying damn-all nothing about it one way or another—to build a boat.

Garth examined the gaunt gray structure that was sheltering us from the sea wind, Frankie close by him in case he needed the Hatchet. He kicked the clapboards, sounded the walls. "This one might do to live in," he said. "And we'll find stuff here and yonder, for the building." Then he and Frankie went inside the place to consider beams, studs, floorboards, the state of the roof, while the rest of us explored the town.

Demetrios was attracted by a heap of rubble where he glimpsed on a charred signboard the letters DWARE. He poked with his oaken stick, uncovering a hammer rusted but not spoiled, with a metal shaft, and a grip still covered by a good-handling material unknown to us. The hardware shop must have been burned before the looting was finished, and its treasure buried from sight under plaster and trash and charcoal. Bosco and Nod helped us. We grubbed and besooted ourselves in the ruin, winning two hand-saws still with a coating of the manufacturer's wax, some barrels of nails, a two-edged ax, an auger with a set of bits, a draw-shave. There was of course much intricate gadgetry that Demetrios recognized as electric, which we tossed aside.

Returning to our house and garden, we found Garth and Frankie already engaged in renovating. The front room possessed an enormous window of heavy glass amazingly unbroken. Other windows, gaping and forlorn, could be boarded up against winter winds, and through the great Old-Time window we could watch the ocean's changes when the sun went down. The chimney was sound, the fireplace in that main room large enough so we could cook there, and the room would also accommodate our sleeping gear. We noticed signs of rats, but after Brand had spent a night or two with the run of the house we heard no more scampering in the walls.

Garth with our loot from the hardware store was a happy man. His happiness spread about him, as light will, touching Blynken with a particular radiance. "With that stuff we can go on a ways," Garth said. "Aye-so, when I'm building I'm right with myself." Later, after his work routines were established, and the mild winter brought certain days of rain when he could not work on the boat, Garth made us more of those small carvings which to him seemed nothing wonderful. For Blynken he carved a swan with lifted wings and she said in the same hour that she hoped Garth would father her next child. It is like that with us; I hope our easiness with one another will continue when the ways of living grow more intricate, as I suppose they must.

Frankie was illuminated with satisfaction too that first day in the town that was probably not Aberedo, when it was decided that certain wall-hooks in the Old-Time kitchen should be sacred to the priceless tools, and that Frankie himself should keep watch of this, empowered to raise hell with anyone who failed to replace them after use— and cleaned too. Angus laid his hands on Frankie's shoulders, and though he may have intended a jest, when he spoke it was in solemn earnest: "From this day forth thou art Toolwarden."

—And that is about the way we have used the old second-person singular ever since—for emphasis, or special events of solemnity like this one, or those astounding occasions when two or three people (possibly even more though I have never known it to happen) not under the urgings of desire or self-importance, are able to share and enter one another's lives however briefly, doing so lovingly and unafraid. It may happen without speech, but not with much depth, for words—the right words, seldom heard— are like no other sort of embrace. That is why the Professor troubles me, though I love him dearly; but on the island Peranelios (which we have so named because the

167

*invention comes from the stories of Demetrios) we never invade the privacy of another with suggestions of how he ought to be doing things this way or that way in the character of somebody else. Yes, your novelist ran on several steps ahead, a bratty thing to do. I am sorry. I only started out to say that Toolwarden is no small status, and nobody could have filled the position more excellently over the years than Frankie—who has yet to write his first book: just wait awhile.*

The boat Garth set himself to build could only be a dignified raft with a sail, a keel, a rudder-sweep, a cabin. Our tools and knowledge offered no way to warp and form the long grand curves of a true ship. It doesn't matter—we knew from the first trials that she would serve. Bosco said she wouldn't float. We launched her, very incomplete, hardly more than a framework platform, to work out a few problems with the steering and the keel, and several times more before Garth was satisfied with the setting of the mast, and she floated nicely, but Bosco wasn't convinced. She wouldn't carry the weight of the cabin, he said, not with all those people.

Bosco's real trouble lay deeper. He just didn't want to gosemplace, not with us anyway. Angus finally took care of it, after the rest of the Company, including Bosco, had wasted considerable time and effort stewing about it—you know, chewing the mahooha in corners with each other, uptight about hurt feelings, ballywambling around. Angus just sat down by Bosco one evening—it was still warm enough so that we were eating some of our meals out in the garden—and said: "You don't really want to go west with us, do you, Bosco?"

"To be real honest with you," says Bosco, "it's a fact I don't. But I wouldn't want to let you down."

"Sooner say good-bye than take you where you don't want to go," said Angus, and he added in his gentle nononsense way just as if he meant it: "We'll miss you naturally."

Maybe he did mean it. Maybe it takes a Ristacrat to lay on just enough butter, never too much, so you're never sure it's butter at all. He never buttered up Demetrios, of course, because he loved him, nor me because he knew

168

I'd have been aware of it. He may have laid it on slightly now and then with quick-tempered Nod, to simmer him down, and with Garth (slower of wit but thin-skinned) for no reason except that he loved to make Garth feel good—name me a better reason and you can have it.

"Since you put it thataway," said Bosco, "and with no hard feelings, I believe I better split. See, it's this thing about Gammo's Ramblers. If they went west a ways from that town T.S. spoke of, they wouldn't've gone far west. Ocean and wilderness don't draw no Ramblers, account they want to find a crowd in between ramblings, sell a few things, have some fun. And anyway it's kind of on me to find Boss Gammo. I don't care so much about he might've been my Pa, but the thing of it is I owe him a licking. Even if he's past seventy-something when I catch up with him he'll still be meaner'n a cat turd, and I'll have to give him—well, a little one. Not, of course, if he can't stand up."

So early next morning Bosco made his farewells, with small gifts from everyone, and the bow Garth had made for him, and new deerhide sandals cut and thonged by Nod's hands, and so forth—we all chipped in. While the rest were occupied with good wishes and flapdoodle I whispered to Frankie to go look at the tools, which he did, and came back to say everything was in place, what was the matter?—in fact he was annoyed with me, for all he loved me so much and still does. (*Oh, now it's out.*) "What was you thinking of, Wynken?" says my Frankie, my Brains of the Outfit. (*But not through your cleverness: through mine, mine.*) "Aye-well," I told him, "I was just wondering."

Not until evening, when Bosco was long gone into the wilderness on his way back to his own kind of life, did Angus miss his wristwatch.

"I must have left it on the Billy-Rock when I went swimming yesterday," said Angus, knowing himself he was never that careless. For we had a little beach, sand-drifted for us by that lazy-seeming ocean, and Angus still liked to run in for a dip after the air had grown too sharp for the rest of us. Near the margin of the beach a statue of some gentleman named William Penn had fallen over or been pushed; it was earthquake country. The old boy now lies gazing at the sky in benignant perplexity.

I went with Angus to help him look. He ran his hand over the pedestal, I poked around here and there; when we gave it up he sat down and laughed. "Oh, that damned roly-poly bastard!" he said, and laughed some more, but he was doing it to hide the fact that he was crying—Angus weeps rather easily; I believe it's better than leaving frustrated unhappiness to fester—and I knew it was because Demetrios that afternoon had let slip an unintentional word during an attack of his sickness. It meant, or at least Angus took it to mean, that Demetrios didn't think he'd live to sail with us when the boat was ready.

"He's had a life," I said, "in two worlds, and there's been pleasure in it."

"You do see into me." (Well, human nature is my country—I have to look where I'm going.) Then Angus struck his knee in misery. "Two worlds—why not three? Why can't he live to glimpse the third world he wants for us, the republic? It's his dream, the rest of us are only groping after his meaning—except maybe you."

"Are you looking for justice in nature?"

"I suppose I was," he said, and his weeping ceased. "He said, you know—it was when the pain had let up, but he was exhausted, near sleep I think, maybe didn't know I was still sitting by him—he muttered something about the Moses principle."

"Maybe he only meant that all prophets are like Moses, because the promised land always stays somewhere just ahead." He didn't answer me, but took my hand and held it against his throat, a way he had, so that I felt his good blood beating there. "The promised land, when we get to ours, will have a few headaches."

"Don't I know, love? But he would enjoy dealing with them. He would ilke to see—ah, I'm going in for a dip." He jumped up and shrugged off his clothes. "Come with me?"

It was too cold, but I did anyway—because he's such a dear hunk of boy, I suppose, with his red-brown hair and his build like a Raphael angel, and I didn't want to leave him. We plunged, and swam a while, and dried in the

170

breeze, and made love. Only in the ways Angus allowed us, because he was afraid for me.

It's true enough a midget would be taking a chance, with no surgeon around to do a Caesarean. Yet I had an easy delivery with Nod's baby—it was sickness that took her —and I was facing almost the same risk in that pregnancy, for we're told midgets don't breed true. But Nod and I are not proportionately short-legged and big-headed: couldn't we be something a little bit new? I wish it were so—and didn't Demetrios himself, on a later afternoon during one of his remissions, say that he wished the Republic might have many people like Nod and me? And didn't we at once fall to designing houses in our heads where big and little could live together and both be comfortable?

She was a very tiny thing, my baby who lived three months, all in such perfect proportion—

I had milk for her, in plenty. Diphtheria killed her— one of the diseases conquered in the Old Time that will not come again.

Nod's wildness is beautiful and strikes a spark in me, but I am partial to gentleness too. Angus is sweet. Eve who had been Solitaire smiled on us without malice out of her young maternity when we went back to the house, quieter and comforted.

Through the early winter we toiled at our vessel under Garth's direction. Winter comes to southern Penn, if that is where we were, only as a chilling of the air for a few months, with seldom a killing frost such as we expected in Lowelltown for December and January. Long rains fall, almost never snow. We were puzzled, what to use for a sail; Demetrios warned us the woolen blankets would be no good, holding damp instead of shedding it. We thought of sending a party back along our trail to the last town we had passed, to buy linen cloth; but it had been a mean, small place, likely with nothing to offer, and Angus was not minded to divide the Company.

Angus himself would not leave Demetrios. He had promised a certain service to his friend that no one else could or should perform. He trusted me with the knowledge of it; since he has given me leave to write it, the others will

171

learn (perhaps without much surprise) when they read what I have set down here, so much later.

As for the sail, we patched our garments together, and cut up the blankets for such small rags of clothing as we might want from time to time. The cabin of the boat was sound enough to hold in our warmth and give us shelter; we would probably be sailing into a region of tropical warmth. We all like nakedness, and we were young.

The Professor (young? well, yes, really, in all that matters) spent most of his time with our friend, studying his face while the lute made music for him, knowing (often without a word from Demetrios) what mood of music the sick man's mind might prefer to follow. He would shift suddenly from joy to sorrow, or the other way, or from simplicity into a counterpoint so subtle that Demetrios would frown with delight in going along with it —all this in response to some message from Demetrios that we had missed. And whatever the shift of mood, Demetrios would nod with satisfaction, and share the journey until the pain struck again destroying the chance of pleasure.

I have not heart nor wish to write of Demetrios's sufferings nor of the thousand indignities that attend a long dying, except to say: he endured them, until the time came when he could tell his beloved that he wished to endure them no more. He did speak once, placidly but with some contempt, of the Old-Time habits of pawky euphemism, of wrapping its human stuff in a bundle of comfort against the facts of death and suffering and finality. And once, when Garth and Frankie and the Professor and I were with him, he said: "I have nothing intricate to tell you about death. Death is necessary, like birth; dying is unpleasant, also unimportant. Except for such truisms, such small obvious bits of comment—why, there's just nothing worth saying about it: it is life that speaks. Play us a little Mozart, Professor—he was a good cheerful joe who knew how to cry."

There came a warm day of March when by unspoken agreement we left Angus alone with him, and lingered outside the house, sometimes looking at our finished boat

172

where she tugged at the anchor bespoken by an easterly breeze.

*You may be wondering certain things. I am writing in the year when Demetrios's dark-haired daughter, Eve's daughter, is seven years old. My sister's girl was born two days later; she is fair and bouncing, and small like Nod and me.*

*As I hinted some long time ago, I returned for a visit to the eastern nations. I traveled in safety, with Garth and a much bigger Frankie. We had a few days in Nuber. Mam Estelle was dead. Babette came back with us, with the Diary, Shawn's pictures, a few other bits of valued loot. It was good to return; it is good to discover the end of this book, and turn my thoughts to other affairs. It will be evening presently, and Eve's daughter Miranda will go to chasing fireflies.*

Out there watching the Inland Sea, we felt no need of saying good-bye, for each time we had been with Demetrios lately it had been a good-bye; he knew it. In an hour, or two, Angus came out of the house and sat on the ground, and when Eve went to him he lifted a handful of earth and let it flow through his fingers.

Afterward he told me how Demetrios had asked after each of us in turn, whether we were of good heart and right with ourselves. "And then he told me," said Angus, "that pain had won, over the enjoyment of living, and so it was time for what we had agreed on. And he said— how could this be, Wynken?—he said that in our short time together he had known more delight of body and mind than he supposed most men ever crowded into a lifetime. Can such a thing be true, Wynken?" he asked me, as if I knew. I don't know in how many senses it can be true. But I think, and I told Angus, that it was certainly the aspect of truth that Demetrios was accepting.

Then Angus had kissed his friend, and placed a cushion over his face and held him fast until it was over, because this was the manner of death that Demetrios had requested, saying there would be no distress in it under Angus's hands, and wishing that Angus might later be free to tell us the whole truth of it or not, as he saw fit.

We had thought to give him a sea burial. But Garth's

good boat carried us more swiftly than we expected to that island we had watched from the mainland. It was lonely and small, a patch of innocent wilderness. Not a place for the republic, but we could pause there, before sailing on to find the island we would name Peranelios, where this part of the story ends. And it suited our hearts to bury Demetrios's body there, near a wild grape that would accept it and bear fruit each season in the sun.

# Edgar Pangborn

## DAVY

DAVY is set in the far future of our world, in the fourth century after the collapse of what we describe as twentieth-century civilisation. In a land turned upside-down and backwards by the results of scientific un-wisdom, Davy and his fellow-Ramblers are carefree outcasts, whose bawdy, joyous adventures among the dead ashes of Old-Time culture make a novel which has been hailed as 'a frightening, ribald, poignant look at an imaginary future,' as 'this chilling and fascinating book,' as 'superb entertainment . . . unique,' as 'so unusual as to make it both refreshing and thought-provoking.'

*70p*

## WEST OF THE SUN

WEST OF THE SUN describes the impact of Man's intrusion into a strange and distant world, a planet the newcomers call Lucifer. Menacing creatures, bizarre plants—and among them two humanoid species involved in mutual strife. What effect will the marooned crew of the space-ship *Argo* have on their unconsenting hosts? 'Man is neither good nor bad, but both,' says one of them. 'But he can swing the balance.'

*60p*

Wyndham Books are obtainable from many booksellers and newsagents. If you have any difficulty please send purchase price plus postage on the scale below to:

Wyndham Cash Sales,
123 King Street,
London W6 9JG

OR

Star Book Service,
G.P.O. Box 29,
Douglas,
Isle of Man,
British Isles

While every effort is made to keep prices low, it is sometimes necessary to increase prices at short notice. Wyndham Books reserve the right to show new retail prices on covers which may differ from those advertised in the text or elsewhere.

1 Book  — 11p
2 Books — 17p
3 Books — 20p
4 Books — 26p
5 Books and over — 30p